Everlasting Love

Bev Haynes

Published by Bev Haynes, 2018.

EVERLASTING LOVE

First edition. July 16, 2018.

Copyright © 2018 Bev Haynes.

ISBN: 979-8230518051

Written by Bev Haynes.

Also by Bev Haynes

Quilted Hills
In Plain Sight
Amish Heritage
One Amish Autumn
My Amish Rose
Amish At Heart

Standalone
Everlasting Love

Table of Contents

CHAPTER 1

There it was. The house sat on a parcel of land jutting out into a river. The glistering water sparkled in the moonlight and reflected its glimmer through the evergreens covering the property.

January slowed the car to a stop on the gravel. She should have left Denver earlier in the day because now, her stomach flipped with uncertainty. Had she taken the right turn after the river bridge? Rummaging around the passenger seat, she grasped the slip of paper with the instructions her lawyer had given her. Switching on the dome light, she reread them, and her heart began to pound. "Something must be wrong," she uttered into the quiet interior of the car. "That big house over there can't be mine. Can it?" The only answer was the gentle purr of the motor idling in the cold, night air.

Twisting around to look at the road behind the car, she could see nothing. All she needed now was to careen into the river. No, the only way out of here was straight ahead. She put the car in gear and eased her way down the dark road. The closer she came to the large house, the closer the lilac bushes drew toward the center of the road that was, at this point, no more than a narrow path. The stiff branches scraped the doors, and she shuddered, dreading to see the damage in the morning light.

What had she been thinking to drive out to the edge of town at night to see her inheritance?

If she made it to the house, she would steer the remains of her car into town and find a nice motel for the night. Just as the thought crossed her mind, she emerged into a clearing at the front of the house. She would explain her late arrival to the real estate agent tomorrow. As it was, she didn't see another vehicle around. He must have given up on her.

January stopped the car and took a deep breath. It felt as if her life had been severed into two distinct segments—before this day and after this day. Her spirit of adventure overcame her desire for security, and she tossed open the door, swung her feet to the ground, and stood in the cold early spring air.

Whoever had named the property really had a flair for words. The title described it perfectly. Pine Gables. January looked up at the gables along the roofline from her vantage point. The house was so compelling...not *the* house, if she were fortunate enough, *her house*! She walked toward it, wishing that she hadn't missed the realtor because she could hardly wait to see inside. Excitement filled her. Wouldn't it be wonderful if this old home really were hers? Could she be that lucky?

Turning, she walked to the back of the house. Here, the remainder of springtime snow showed in tall snow drifts as she picked her way around them, walking toward the heavy, wooden door. Probably, it would be locked, but if it weren't, she would go inside and look around. Besides, she was getting cold, and her teeth gently chattered as she breathed.

The steps leading to the door were in terrible shape. As January ascended the stairs, she felt the first one give under the pressure of her weight. The moonlight illuminated the next rotting board showing it wasn't attached on one side. So much for going inside the mansion. Her spirits sank. January returned to the cold ground to finish the trek around the house when a light shining from a basement window caught her attention. She raced over to it, dropped to her knees and, by placing either hand beside her face, peered into the room.

"Oh!" she cried aloud into the crisp night air, not believing her eyes. It couldn't be...

"I caught you at last, you—you vandal!"

January didn't have time to protect herself or so much as force a scream for help. Suddenly, she was face down on the ground, her slight frame pushed into the wet spring snow like a candy decoration on a whipped-cream frosted cake.

She struggled to free herself, but the more she moved, the harder her captor pushed his shoulders into her back. Kicking her leg out with all the power she could muster, her foot connected with his side.

"Ouch, you little witch! I should tan your hide." He loosened his hold of her.

Taking advantage of her momentary freedom, January struggled to her feet and nearly fell. Her legs felt numb, not only from the fall, but from absolute terror. Snapping her head to the side, she surveyed the area for an escape route. The wall of the rock mansion was on one side of her and lilac bushes on the other. She jumped toward the bushes, but the man was quicker. He sprang to his feet in one graceful movement, grabbed her around the shoulders, and pulled her back against him.

January's mind spun, but she couldn't find an escape route. What in heaven was she going to do now? "Let go of me!" she shrieked, her voice cracking with hysteria.

"First, I'm calling the sheriff," the man huffed, his breath filled with anger. He whirled her around and pushed her against the rock wall. The thick undergrowth caught at her wool skirt and scraped her legs.

January's heart sank. The man was wild with rage. The whites of his eyes glistened in the moonlight, and his face contorted crazily. Dressed in black jeans, blood-red shirt, and an ominous black, western-style duster that flapped in the wind like a predatory bird, he resembled–a vampire. She shuddered as thick clouds engulfed the moon deepening the shadows cast by the vast mansion. January's stomach contracted, and bile filled her throat. Her captor held her with one hand and, reaching inside his duster, retrieved a cellular telephone. "You're staying right here until the sheriff arrives."

So much for thinking he was a reanimated corpse. In all her years of reading horror novels, never once had a vampire used a phone! His words made her swallow hard. At least he was calling the police. "B-but you don't understand!" she cried. Panic pounding at the base of her skull eradicated her powers of reason, and the sharp rock of the stone wall bit into her back as she tried to squirm from his grasp.

"Oh, I understand all right. I've been trying to catch you for over a month. You—you teenagers!"

"Let go of me! Now!" Her mouth twisted in anger.

"Say now, you're a real spit-fire."

Suddenly, her body trembled under his gaze, anxiety mingled with her anger. What was he talking about? What did this man think she'd done? She had to do something even if her situation seemed dismal. Instinctively, she stomped her foot down hard on the top of his instep

"Ouch! Do that again and I-I'll—" A nasty grin pulled at the corners of his full lips showing a row of ultra-white teeth. No fangs protruded to tear at her creamy white throat. "I guess I'm lucky you're such a little bit of a thing or else you could have broken my foot." He leaned a forearm against her shoulders and holding the phone in the other hand, dialed.

His gore-colored shirt collar tickled her nose when he moved. Her heart pounded against the confining bone structure in her chest. "No. Wait...you don't understand" January whispered, her energy drained from the struggle. "I think I might own this place. I'm here to meet a real estate broker." Defeated, she sagged against him. As her chest pressed against his, an electrical charge surged through her, taking with it the little breath she had left.

Suddenly, the tension seemed to evaporate from her captor; she felt his muscles contract, then go slack like a rubber band snapping from too much stress. Had he felt the electricity also? He took a step back, releasing her from his grasp. "Ms. Mohr?" His square jaw throbbed as he stared at her, his heated gaze boring into hers.

"H-How do you know my name?"

The faint sound of someone at the other end of the telephone caught his attention, and he looked bewilderedly at her, then returned his concentration back to the phone. "Sorry. Wrong number," he uttered into the phone. Snapping it shut, he dropped it into his duster pocket. Tentatively, the corners of his mouth edged upward and transformed his sneer into a dazzling smile. "Did we have an appointment?" He offered her his hand.

The man's arrogance irritated her. Slapping away his outstretched hand, she watched it drop to his side. "You're Mr. Cottier?"

He slowly nodded.

"Well, you scared the hell out of me! Why did you attack me?" Her bright green eyes narrowed and snapped with anger. "It was bad enough seeing that..."

"Seeing what?" he asked turning his head to survey the area. "Did you see the kids that have been tearing up the place?"

Stalling for time, she wiped a thin film of perspiration from her forehead with her gloved hand. She needed a second to catch her breath. "I-In the basement. I-I was looking for you when I saw a shadow on the window. It must have been you." She bit her tongue, disgusted with herself. This was the biggest lie of her life, but she couldn't tell him what she really had seen in the basement. He would think her mad if she told him she had seen—a ghost.

"How'd you get here?" he asked, looking around for her means of transportation, then he reached out to straighten her stocking hat sitting awkwardly on her white-blonde hair.

January stepped back from him not from fear, but from his magnetic aura. Her body seemed to betray her as she yearned for this stranger's touch, an absurd situation but there just the same. "I drove my car, it's in the driveway on the other side of the house."

"Let's go," he said, firmly grasping her elbow to assist her around the side of the mansion.

Jerking her arm out of his hand, she quickly stepped away from him. The way her mindless body was reacting, she didn't want him to touch her again. This man was too demanding and forceful. What was the matter with him, anyway?

"Look, Miss Mohr..." He reached out and touched her again, turning her to face him. At once his irritation evaporated, and his eyes seemed to soften. She knew he'd seen the tears in her eyes.

"Hey, I'm not going to hurt you. I just thought you were a prowler. I've had some problems lately with kids breaking into the house, I just assumed..."

"Do I look like a kid?"

His eyes raked over her. "Well, now that you mention it." He looked away from her, trying to hide his lopsided grin, but she saw it anyway. It annoyed her that he found this even a little bit funny.

She sighed. There was no sense in getting riled. This man seemed pleasant enough now that he knew who she was. "So tell me, why you didn't meet me earlier?"

He shook his head, dismayed. "I didn't know you were coming. I left a message with your lawyer, you were supposed to call me first."

"This is such a mess. I did call last week."

"Come on, let's get out of the cold and sort this out later."

January gave a sideways glance at the window where she'd seen...the ghost. She wanted to look in there again. Surely, she hadn't really seen it. The notion made her shudder as fingers of fear fluttered down her spine. Keeping her head down, she turned away from the house and walked into the wind. As they tramped through the tall weeds, she watched her escort from the corner of her eye.

The clouds moved across the night sky and were illuminated by the moon. Its white light filtered through the evergreen trees and a patch shown on Ben Cottier. His dark hair blew away from his face exposing his straight hairline and wisps of gray sparkled at his temples. He wore his hair long in the back. A mullet? It was an old-fashioned style, but it looked good on him. It added to his masculine appearance. He towered over her diminutive frame. Everyone, it seemed, towered over her, and she guessed him to be over six-feet tall, a full foot taller than she. There was no doubt; the man with whom she'd wrestled on the ground was deadly handsome.

He looked so self-assured and confident. January found it hard to remain angry with him.

This man oozed sex appeal and that spelled trouble in capital letters.

Emerging at the driveway, Ben walked with her to the car and opened the door. "I have to make this terrible mistake up to you somehow," he said, planting his fist on the top of the car, trapping her between his arm and the open car door. "Can we have coffee? There's a place that shouldn't be too crowded at this hour. We can talk about this?"

A grin played at the corners of his wide, full mouth. He didn't look quite so terrifying now; actually, his crooked grin gave his face a boyish quality. His nearness and his woodsy aroma made her dizzy. Overpowered by a wave of desire, she wondered how his kisses would feel against hers. Taking a shuddering breath, she tried to focus her thoughts on something less erotic.

"Actually, I'm cold, and my muscles are beginning to get tight from that fall I took." She eased herself into the seat and pulled her legs into the interior of the car. "I'm starving."

"I can't begin to tell you how sorry I am for hurting you," he spoke intently, then leaned closer to her. "I'll ride with you. I don't have my vehicle with me." He didn't wait for her answer; he just walked around the small car, jerked open the door and plopped down into the passenger seat.

January glanced over at him, and then reached under her seat to search for the keys pushing candy wrappers and pop cans out of the way. "Sorry about the mess. It was a long drive from Denver. I ate to stay alert." She grasped her key ring and felt the attached round crystal. "You'll have to point the way because I can't see where to drive. Is it always so dark around here?" she asked, trying to gather her wits. She peered into the darkness as she pushed against the steering wheel to tighten her muscles. The isometric exercise usually relaxed her, but not this night.

"Head toward the pines on the right side of the house," he said, leaning forward in the seat to stare into the dark. He studied the driveway as she started the car, switched on the lights and shifted into first gear.

"Over there," he said, pointing. "Turn when you get to the lone evergreen."

In response to his direction, she maneuvered the car around the circular driveway. The car lights danced through the trees making an eerie play of shadows against the house. Neither of them looked back as they drove away. A dense shadow fell across a third-floor window and materialized into a silhouette of a woman. It seemed to be watching as the car disappeared into the grove of trees.

THE DOWNTOWN AREA OF Garrison, Wyoming, was only two blocks long. Pulsing neon announced the Garrison Grill nestled between a bank on one side and a bar on the other. Strains of country music spilled from the bar. If the cars parked in front of the buildings were any indication, the bar commanded the most business. She could see a flower shop, the post office and numerous small businesses down the narrow street. This town was so different from Denver where even the smallest suburb was a riot of noise and activity. She never wanted to live in rural America because she had always assumed it would be boring. Apparently, she was right.

January stepped out of the car. The smell of burgers and fries assaulted her senses, and her stomach growled in response. Even candy and pop wore off after a while. "I didn't realize I was hungry," she said, following Ben to the entrance.

He opened the battered wooden door for her and hung their coats on the aluminum coat tree. January pulled her hat from her head and stuffed it into the sleeve of her jacket. As she walked to the back of the café, she felt the patrons' eyes follow her with that small-town look of curiosity. She hadn't attempted to tidy her hair after removing the hat; she must look quite a mess after her long drive and her wrestling match with Ben. "I'm happy you suggested coming here," she offered soothingly. She caught a glimpse of herself in a mirror hanging over the salad bar. Her cropped, white-blond hair stood on end and was filled with static. She ran her fingers through the spiky softness in an attempt to make it behave. "I wasn't dressed for anywhere more formal." Ben looked at her quizzically. She sensed he was struggling to say something but had changed his mind. The smell of food made her stomach roar with hunger. "When I made up my mind that I really was going to drive up here, I called my parents to ask them to watch my apartment, and then I took off."

Ben stared absently, his thoughts guarded, at the dark paneled wall across the room. "I'm sure you'll feel better after you eat."

"I'll just bet you're right."

Leaning on her elbows, she folded her hands and rested her chin on her knuckles. "How large is this town? We only drove a few blocks and," she looked around, "here we are."

Returning his attention to January, Ben smiled causing the small lines around his eyes to deepen. "Garrison has nine hundred good folks and six sore heads. In which category do I place you?" His eyes grew wide, and he continued, "no, no, don't answer that one. After everything I've put you through, I shouldn't ask an open question like that."

"I'll answer you in a few days. I haven't decided, yet." She laughed softly, and the change of the mood fed warmth into the knot in her stomach and relaxed.

"Now that I see you in the light, I can't believe I mistook you for a prowler," he said sincerely, shaking his head.

"And I can't believe I thought you were a vampire! You can't know how frightened I was to see your wings flapping at me when you attacked!"

"Vampire?"

"Your dark duster...with the wind billowing it the way it was. Y-you looked like a demon from hell."

"Oh! Now I get it...I'm so sorry for that. When I saw your exotic eyes hurling machetes at me, I was afraid, too."

That was strange; she had noticed his eyes, too.

The waitress poured the coffee and January took a sip of hot, aromatic liquid and allowed it to slowly trickle down her throat and warm her from the inside out. "Um, that feels better."

Ben reached into his pocket and brought out a pair of glasses. He slipped them on and scanned the menu. When the waitress returned, they ordered. He studied January's face, then asked, "So tell me, why are you really here?"

"I wanted to see the estate because, if it's livable, I'm going to move into the house." There. It was out in the open. She said the words aloud at last. Ben's dark eyes grew wide, and he raked his fingers through his hair, leaving glossy ridges. He remained silent for a time, then slumped in the booth. "Whew, that's different. The house hasn't been lived in, in years. Why did it take you so long to come here?"

"I had a lot to digest. First, on New Year's Day, my birthday, I had a meeting with my parents and an attorney. Can you imagine that? A lawyer working on a holiday, anyway, I learned that I was adopted...and about the inheritance." She lowered her eyes and looked at the steaming coffee. "At first I wanted to sell the estate, take the money and go on an extended vacation to a warm island paradise."

"What stopped you?"

She shrugged. "I really don't know. I have a profession, it doesn't pay well, but I'm good at it. It was a difficult decision to make."

"So, you were born in January. Is that the reason for your unusual name?" Tapping his fingers on the table, he stared at her for a long moment as she nodded. "Why not sell? You can put the money into anything you want."

January shook her head. Why was he pushing her? "No. That doesn't interest me."

"Miss Mohr, it doesn't pay to be stubborn and obstinate. He looked at her over the top of his glasses. "You say you're going to live in that huge house. Tell me the rest of it. What are you going to do with the house, turn it into a bed and breakfast?"

"First of all, I'm not upset." But anger churned within her. She had no intention of putting his fears at ease just yet.

"Oh, really? If you're not upset, why is the muscle in your jaw throbbing?" Ben asked sarcastically.

She felt her face flush with embarrassment. How could Ben read her so quickly when they had only met ninety short minutes ago? She was tired of taking orders from supervisors that didn't really care about the residents she nursed so lovingly?

She was a nurse at the Eventide Nursing Home. Nursing had been her career for the last eight years, and she loved the old people, but the stress of watching their failing health was becoming too much for her, emotionally. She wanted to do something new. Something she could put many hours into, be her own boss, reap the benefits from her hard work. And there was something more. She needed to be in a location where she was free to let her creativity soar.

"January?" Ben's voice brought her back.

"Oh! I'm sorry. What did you say?" She blinked her eyes to clear the fog from her mind.

Ben shook his head and smiled. "I didn't hear from your lawyer. Are you sure he called me?"

"Well...he said he talked to a Mr. Bennett Cottier."

"Oh." He paused, taking the last swallow of his coffee. "It's possible that your lawyer spoke to my father. That would explain the mix-up." His deep-set eyes softened as he looked at her. "I'm really sorry about the way we met."

She smiled, the tension that knotted her shoulders eased as she took in his sincere gaze. "It's OK. But I think we're going to have another problem. You, or whomever Mr. Livingston talked to, was supposed to have made a reservation for me at..." She fumbled through her purse looking for her note with all the information scribbled across it.

Ben tapped his index finger against his chin as he considered her situation. "Since we suspect that the lawyer talked to my father, it won't matter where you stay because I'm sure he didn't make the reservation."

"See, a problem," January said.

"Well, it's not much of one at this time of the year. There isn't anything going on around here to bring people to Garrison this early in the spring." He reached into his duster pocket, fumbled a bit and took out his phone. "The only problem with these things," he said, "is not having a phone book." He unfolded his long legs from the booth and stood. "I'll be right back." He walked to the entrance of the kitchen and disappeared.

While he was gone, January looked around the quaint café. It was scrupulously clean and well maintained. There were many tables, mostly filled, and the patron's appeared to know each other as they talked to diners' across from them. She searched to find something to dislike, but, like it or not, she felt comfortable here in Garrison even if it was a quiet, little town.

Then she noticed the way the women were dressed. Most of them had on work worn Wrangler jeans, and boots. January looked down at her baggy attire. She must look foreign to them in her long skirt and indigo cotton sweater. In fact, she had observed Ben looking quizzically at her when she had removed her coat earlier.

Ben slid into the booth just as the waitress brought their meal. "They'll put you up at the Sidewinder." He stacked the tomato, pickle, and lettuce on the breaded meat and covered the bun with catsup.

"Sidewinder? Is that on a ranch?" Her heart sank at the dreadful thought. Staying in this small town would take some adjustment, but staying in a Sidewinder? Images of snakes, sagebrush, and rocks popped into her mind.

Ben laughed at January's horrified expression. "No...no, the Sidewinder is a motel down the street. And it's the most modern motel in town. The others are old and outdated. The Sidewinder is fashionably western. Some of the area artists donated their western paintings for the rooms. It's really quite nice, I hear. Then again, it might not compare to Denver."

"I don't care about that. I just hope it's not too expensive. Maybe I should stay in an older motel."

Ben shook his head slightly. "You won't need to pay for anything. Charge everything to me and I will bill the estate. I'm the executor of the property. As soon as the paperwork is done, you will have a lot of money to work with."

She looked at him over the edge of her coffee cup as she took a sip. "Isn't that unusual for a broker?"

Ben shrugged. "I guess. It's a complicated story, but to simplify...I inherited part of the estate myself...the ranch."

This bit of information excited her, and she reached over and caught his hand. He was part of this! She wasn't alone floundering for facts. "Who is this benefactor?" she asked excitedly.

"I don't know, and I've tried to find out, but it's still a mystery to me." He recanted searching the records at the courthouse only to find the records had been sealed for twenty-nine years. "I'm selling out. Large ranches with a lot of deeded land are prime property and very seldom last long enough to get listed. Anyway, your lawyer asked me to oversee the remainder of the estate. You own the estate now that the contract with the state is up. And I have been chasing vandals for you."

"I really didn't know you were involved in all of this," she said sincerely. She dipped a fry in catsup and nibbled thoughtfully.

Ben stared at her. "You don't know, do you?"

"Know what?"

"Damn! Here I've been thinking you only wanted the money and you..." he trailed off.

"I wish you would finish your thoughts. I haven't the foggiest idea what you're rambling about." She pushed another French fry in her mouth.

"Jan, look at me."

Her eyes widened in surprise. No one had ever shortened her name. She'd never thought of herself as Jan. But she liked it. "What is it?" Curiosity edged her voice.

"The house has been empty for thirty years."

"Oh goodness, it must be a complete disaster." She felt her heart sink. How would she find the money to do this? She hadn't thought the house would be neglected and vacant for so many years. "

"Don't look so glum, Jan. There has been enough money to keep the house in good repair. It's still filled with treasures...but I can hardly bear the thought of you opening it to guests. Please tell me you aren't going to turn it into a bed and breakfast."

"Okay, I'll tell you that I'm not planning to turn it into a bed and breakfast." She smiled at him.

Ben grimaced. "Say that with some sincerity, and I'll believe you."

"Have you been in the mansion?"

"A few times," Ben offered, his tone guarded.

His tentative tone made her wonder if he had glimpsed the ghost during some of his business visits to the house?

"When I was waiting for you earlier, I saw something in a basement window I thought it was," Her voice trailed away as she said, "a...ghost."

CHAPTER 2

W hat?" he asked, his brows knitted together in question.

"I know, you think I've lost it, and you may be right."

"A ghost. You really think you saw a ghost?"

She didn't reply. She couldn't say the words aloud again.

Ben took a deep breath and turned his gaze to the table. He watched his fingers as he scratched at a dried speck of catsup. "I haven't seen anything like that, but I'll grant you, inside the house, it's oppressively stale. Can you describe what you saw?" he asked and raised his gaze to look at her directly into the eyes.

"It looked like an old woman dressed in calico, but I could see through her. I felt she let me see her. Oh, Ben, this house is perfect for me. I feel like it has been waiting for me all of my life...like I'm coming home to my roots." Passion and excitement filled her voice.

"You frighten me, January." His gaze reverted to the red streaks of catsup on his plate. "Let's not talk about this any longer. We have other business to discuss."

"What now?" she asked, a note of fatigue edging her voice. He was deliberately trying to change the subject. She wanted to know why.

"I hired Jim and Cathy Clark to work as caretakers of the place, but you have the option to reject this arrangement. There's a lot to do around the property, and I sure don't have the time to devote to the project."

"They can stay. I'll need their help if I am to open by June."

"You told me you weren't changing it into a bed and breakfast!"

"I'm not."

"Would you please quit fiddling with my mind? What are you doing with the house?"

"It's a fantastic area for..."

"Oh come on! What?"

"A writer's retreat."

"That's nearly the same thing," Ben shouted. When some of the café customers looked their way, he lowered his voice to an angry whisper with his face turning red. "You can't be serious! No one has lived there for nearly thirty years."

January raised her chin in defiance. "I love challenges, especially when I have money to work with." She knew she was coming across as rebellious and greedy, but Ben Cottier was a powerful, handsome man and January had to prove to him she could be strong and a little nasty if need be.

Ben stood and tossed money on the table for a tip. "Come on. I'll take you to the motel."

She slid from the booth. Her legs felt much steadier now—the food did the trick, but she shivered as Ben touched her shoulder as he guided her to the cash register. January knew there was an overwhelming chemical reaction between them. She had never felt this attracted to a man and it frightened her.

"Mr. Cottier...here you are! We couldn't find you to return your vehicle." A young woman burst through the cafe door. A tall, slim man followed her. His open, flannel shirt covered a dark T-shirt and flapped against his bony hip as he walked. "We came back at the time you said, but you weren't there!"

"Jim...Cathy, here's someone I'd like you to meet." Ben turned toward January. "This is your employer, January Mohr. I caught a ride with her."

Jim stuck out his hand out and grasped hers. His enthusiasm made up for his wife's apathy. "Glad to meet ya, glad to meet ya," he said, pumping her hand. "We're really tickled Mr. Cottier here thought of hirin' us. We just went to his office to find a house to rent and him being a nice guy and all figured we couldn't afford one right now, so he told us about this job."

"Do you two want something to eat or drink?" Ben interrupted in an attempt to shut up the man. "We could talk business while you eat."

"Well, sure, we haven't had anything for a while, Cathy here made us some goulash, but it was a bit pasty, it was a good thing too cuz it's been a while since we ate," Jim said ignoring his wife's reaction, but by the look in Cathy's eyes, January could tell the young woman was ticked.

They all returned to the booth, the young couple sitting on the other side of Ben and January. After the Clark's ordered, January asked, "Have you been working at the mansion very long?"

"Naw. We only took the job just today, that's where we were. Mr. Cottier here was good enough to loan us his vehicle to go see the place. Sorry, but we took advantage of using your vehicle and went for groceries...and we're just gettin' back from there. Pine Gables is really somethin'. I can't wait to start clearin' that brush away from the house. It makes the place look dark and spooky, y'know." He shuddered. January blinked hard trying to keep from staring at Jim. He didn't seem to run out of air.

"Are you going to work at that mansion?" A customer sitting at the table beside them joined the conversation. When the couple slowly nodded in unison, the man's bellowing voice cracked through the drone of diners, "Hot damn! People are movin' into the haunted house. If that don't beat all! You too, Missy?" He looked directly at January.

He held her in his gaze until she answered. "Yes. I'm the owner, *part owner*." A blush crawled up her neck then flamed at her cheeks. She felt as if all the people in the café had turned to stare at her. The silence hung in the air for seconds, and then the diners began to return to their meals and private conversations. The man shrugged and returned his attention to the thick steak that overlapped his plate.

"What is he talking about, Ben?"

Ben closed his eyes and sighed. "I didn't want to get you all shook-up."

"Holy shit! We're going to live in a haunted house? You didn't tell us nuthin' about no ghosts and that kind of stuff. I think we might need to talk about a raise here if you want us to be ghostbusters or some such thing."

Cathy sat in the corner of the booth with her legs pulled under her and suddenly slammed her hand on the table. "Shut the hell up, Jim and let Mr. Cottier talk."

January felt her eyes grow round. The woman didn't say much, but then how could she with Jim's talent for holding his breath for what seemed minutes at a time.

"Come on everyone, no need to get shook up. You know how people are, they need something to talk about," Ben said. "Besides, I've been in there plenty of times and never have I seen a ghost."

"Ever been there all night?" Cathy asked.

"Uh, no." Ben avoided looking at her.

"Well, that's reassuring." Cathy looked up and smiled at the waitress who waited to take their order.

Ben slid out of the booth and took January's hand and pulled her out. "Jim...Cathy, go ahead and order anything you want." He slipped some money from his wallet and handed it to the waitress. "Keep whatever is left for your tip." Returning the conversation to the new caretakers, he said, "Keep the SUV tonight and let's meet tomorrow morning and we'll go through the house. No sense worrying about this. I need to get January settled for the night, so we'll see you both tomorrow."

FOLLOWING BEN'S DIRECTIONS, January steered her car into the parking lot of the Sidewinder Motel. Learning her way around Garrison was going to be easy, January thought. From what she could tell, the town formed a square, about ten blocks in all four directions.

She glimpsed her watch. It was getting late. She had told her parents earlier in the day that she would call when she arrived safely. They would be worrying about her if she didn't contact them soon. Her mom had tendencies to overreact, and January wouldn't be surprised it the state troopers had an all-points bulletin out describing her car as she stood here. There was no sense worrying about it because there was nothing she could do about it until she checked-in.

The building exterior had a rustic appearance, weathered boards covered the main lodge. A wooden walkway led to rough-hewn doors that opened to an interior that showcased a new rendition of the old style. Stepping out of the car, she followed Ben into the lobby. Appalled, January looked around. A stone fireplace dominated one wall, and stuffed animal heads were scattered around the other walls. The trophies had glass eyes that seemed to follow her every movement. She didn't want to look—she didn't want to think about these animals last moments.

Ben gazed around the room. "I've never been in here before, only driven by." He whistled softly under his breath as he looked around. "This is outstanding!"

Shaking her head in disbelief that anyone could think this great, January walked to the check-in counter to complete the necessary arrangements. How could he be so impressed with a room filled with dead animal heads staring at them from their grotesque perches on the wood clad walls?

The middle-aged desk clerk slid the registration toward Ben and took his credit card. When the woman wasn't preoccupied watching a rerun of House Hunters on the television, she gave January accusing looks. The old biddy thought she was having a clandestine romance with Ben. January smiled to herself and accepted the room key. She'd only been in Garrison couple of hours, and she was going to gain a reputation as a wanton eccentric. This was much more fun than her quiet, boring life in Denver.

She and Ben drove the car around the building and found a vacant space in front of Room 20. She pushed a button on the dash that released the latch on the trunk. "You go open the door, and I'll grab your luggage," Ben said as he eased himself out of the seat and walked to the back of the car. "Hey! What's this? Why do you have only one suitcase and a dress bag with you? You are so different from most of the women I've known. With them, a forklift would have been helpful!"

Warm air rushed out of the room as she pushed the door open and then flipped the light switch. Had Ben ushered many women into motel rooms she wondered? She supposed he had, a man as handsome as Ben Cottier could have any woman that he wanted.

"What do you think?" Ben asked strolling around the room, studying it in detail.

"It's better than I expected. I was afraid there would be empty eyes staring at me from the walls!"

He turned around and looked at her. "Weren't they great? Do you realize how much the trophies must have cost? They'd be stolen if they weren't guarded."

"You can't be serious, they're disgusting!" Her nose wrinkled with repulsion.

"Not into rustic, huh?" He said as a genuine smile spread from his lips to his eyes. It reflected his tendency toward humor as he walked to the clothing rack and put her suitcase on the luggage rack.

A series of high-pitched tones filled the room. Ben reached to his side and depressed a button on top of a black pager. "We have a report of a 10-50 PI on Highway 25...mile marker 31." The dispatcher repeated the message.

January dropped onto the bed and stared at Ben. His lean body seemed to change before her eyes. He flipped open his phone and punched in a series of numbers. This had been the strangest day. She felt confused and entirely out of her element, and, for a moment, wondered if she was out of her mind as well.

"EMT 3...ETA Fire Hall 4 minutes," he replied tensely. He listened for a moment then turned toward her saying, "Oh, man...I forgot...Jim and Cathy have my vehicle until tomorrow morning. Can I use your car? I'll drop it by here when I get back and leave the keys at the office." He hesitated for a moment and looked at her expectantly.

She tossed him the keys.

"Thanks," he said as he flew out the door.

Standing in the open doorway, she watched as he ran for the car.

He unlocked the door and hollered at her, "I'll meet you at the estate tomorrow around ten, OK?" January nodded and waved as he raced her car from the lot, throwing loose gravel and dust in every direction.

BEN STEPPED OUT OF January's car. The night sky was clear, and the wind had come up, now it was howling making the night bitterly cold for April. He pulled his hat over his ears and tugged the collar of his coat higher onto his neck to keep out the icy wind. The strong blasts pelted his body and made his walk to the bar difficult. He stuffed the car keys into his pants pocket.

He leaned into the wind keeping his eyes averted. As he walked, he stared down at the rock-littered parking lot. If you lived in Wyoming, you knew how to avoid dust flying into your eyes from the nearly ever-present wind.

HE'D ONLY WALKED A short distance, but the wind sucked the air from his lungs causing him to feel winded. Jerking open the heavy glass door, he entered the dark bar. Ben pulled off his leather, Aussie-style cowboy hat and ran his fingers through his dark hair trying to fix the damage the hat and the wind had caused. Removing his hat was second nature. His first-grade teacher had given his class a lesson in hat etiquette. It was a lesson not easily forgotten.

Finding an empty spot in the noisy bar was easy on weeknights, and he slid onto the nearest booth. Above each table was a wooden rail with pegs to hold the patrons' cowboy hats and Ben tossed his onto the rack beside the others.

"What'll you have?" The bartender called to him from behind the bar in a monotone voice that was barely audible above the country music pouring from the jukebox.

"Just a beer...tap is fine," Ben pushed his glasses up the bridge of his nose. "How have you been doing, Ed?"

"Good, good. Did ya go on the run t'night?"

Ben nodded reluctantly. Here we go again. Being an EMT had disadvantages. It seemed the gruesome details interested and enthralled everyone, and yet giving information was strictly against departmental policy.

"What happened?"

"There was a rollover east of town."

The bartender glanced at the customers as someone whistled sharply in response to winning the game. He kept his head turned from Ben then asked, "Who'd ya take?"

Ben shook his head. He had known that question was coming. Didn't these people ever learn? They wouldn't want everyone in the community talking about them if they'd had a medical emergency. He raised his eyes to look at the man standing beside the table. "I can't say...you...know, confidentiality."

"Yeah, I know how it is," he muttered and walked back toward the bar.

His beer went down smoothly, and he motioned to the bartender to bring him another. He wanted to drown his emotions and be alone tonight. It indeed hadn't gone the way he'd planned. Yesterday, he had invited his ex-fiancée, Audra Lowrey to dinner. This morning, she'd called him and refused his invitation. Ben wondered if her refusal was related to his suggestion of eating pizza instead of a fancy prime rib dinner at the country club. He knew it had been a stupid move on his part because she favored the atmosphere of a nightclub where she could dress lavishly and be seen, no, more like envied by the right people.

Savoring his third beer, wondered how he'd let himself get involved with Audra, let alone engaged to such a conniving woman. They were nothing alike. He was levelheaded and liked to sprawl around the house in sweats reading the newspaper and listening to country music. Audra wore expensive negligees, sipped white wine and enjoyed classical music.

Ben took a long swallow of beer. He relished living in his log house–a few miles west of Garrison–on the lake with a boat dock nearby. The small community was friendly, and he had a fondness for piloting his friends on his ski boat across Garrison Lake in the summer. Audra wanted to live in the city, build a mega-dollar house and throw fancy dinner parties to impress all of her materialistic girlfriends.

Ed returned with another mug of beer. "Thanks. This is it for me." He handed the bartender a bill, then lifted the drink from the rough wood table and placed the cold glass against his forehead. He now realized the relationship with Audra was built on habit more than love and that it had become stale and boring. Two weeks ago, they had a massive fight about where they would live after their marriage. In the end, they broke their engagement. In anger, he'd told her to take a hike and find another sucker to support her wannabe lifestyle.

He wasn't ready, maybe he would never be prepared to marry Audra. She and his father had become very close. Maybe his father was a better match for her. They were both devious, and they both thought Ben was a loser just because he tried to help others instead of using them for his own means. Neither of them understood a thing about character. Ben pushed the nearly empty mug away from him. He laughed aloud. Dad and Audra just might be workable! He stood, took his hat from the rack and walked to the door. Yes, maybe this was the answer to his problem. He definitely would try his skills as a matchmaker. If Dad were busy with beautiful, money hungry Audra, he'd be too busy to interfere with the company.

Ben ran the family's real estate business from two offices, one in Garrison, the other in Wyland. He traveled between five small communities and two larger towns. Ben was busy, but his work also gave him financial freedom. He made a lot of money from the business.

Ben's biggest problem was his father. The man was pompous, arrogant and he was always trying to open doors by working behind the scenes. All his father had to do was show up at the office to make him instantly seethe with anger. As far as the missed communication with January, his father must have intercepted her lawyer's call, which was the only explanation that made sense. Ben needed to find the time...no, make the time to discuss this situation with January Mohr. He wanted to dump that spooky old house in a hurry, but January innocence attracted him, and he'd hate to make an enemy of her.

JANUARY SLOWLY OPENED her eyes and looked around the dim, unfamiliar room trying to remember where she was. The red numbers on the alarm clock brought her back from the deep sleep. A Garrison, Wyoming motel. She stretched and yawned, then turned on her side before throwing her legs over the edge of the bed and sat up, letting the covers fall to her waist. Glancing at the large mirror across the room, she saw her light bangs caught in her dark eyelashes. She brushed them from her face.

"Ouch!" she cried as she moved her arm. A sharp pain radiated through her shoulder. The fall. When Ben upended her, he'd done more damage than she had first thought. Tossing back the covers, she got out of bed and walked to the mirror. Switching on the desk lamp, she grimaced when she saw the angry bruise covering the upper portion of her arm. Turning a bit, she twisted her body to see her shoulder. It was dark and tender as well.

She needed a hot shower and range of motion exercise to limber her muscles. When nursing home residents fell, their physicians ordered exercises once they knew there were no broken bones. Circling her arm over her head, she plopped down on the bed. She had to call her parents. She promised to call last night, but with so much going on, she had forgotten. She reached for the telephone.

After the call, January took her toiletries to the bathroom, slipped off her silky floral robe and stepped into the warm shower spray. She slathered a rich conditioner on her thick blonde hair and leaned back against the wet ceramic tile letting the water beat against her sore shoulder. Her life had changed so much in three short months, her thirtieth birthday having been the pivotal point for the changes. Now, she wanted to make the mansion into a beautiful writer's retreat.

She loved writing short stories and dreamed about writing an historical novel in a vacuum of loneliness that very few people understood. The solitude, the isolation could be so oppressive. Having a place where she could join other writers on her publication quest was a dream that she could soon work at. The mansion...oh, it just had to be beautiful...and the small town added to the charm. She felt this dream really could come true, here and only here, in this delightful community.

Someone was beating on her door. "Hold on," she called out, poking her head around the bathroom door. January quickly turned off the water, and then dried herself. She threw on her robe, looped the sash, and then twisted the thick towel around her head. Peeking out between the vertical blinds, she saw Ben Cottier pacing back-and-forth impatiently. Apparently, Mr. Cottier didn't like to wait.

January's heartbeat increased just knowing he was outside her door. "Good morning," she said as she opened the door a crack, trying to hide behind it.

Ben lost his anxious demeanor and smiled. "Are you going to let me in, or what?"

January looked down at the way she was dressed and tightly pulled the edges of the robe around her body, then tossed open the door. "Come on in," she said happily as her heart thumped excitedly.

Ben's eyes traveled over her in a slow caress when he realized she had nothing on but the sheer robe.

Her breath caught in her chest. What was this man doing to her? She was enjoying standing in front of him without heavy clothing. His gaze softened. Her skin tingled as if he had traced the path with his fingertip over her body, and she savored the erotic sensation as a pulsing spread from her center and shuddered up her spine.

"Looks like I caught you at a bad time," he spoke softly.

"What are you doing here so early?" she asked glancing around the parking lot. She pulled him into the room and closed the door. *Damn, but he was drop-dead gorgeous.*

He tipped his head as he looked at her. "I stopped by city hall to have the electricity turned on.

"At eight thirty? People are working at this time of the day?"

"Yeah…?"

"This sure isn't the big city."

"Thank God," he whispered under his breath. "I have a meeting this tonight, so I thought we'd better get started early. It's cold and damp out today, so you'd better wear something warmer than…uh, warmer than you had on last night. I'd suggest jeans and a sweater."

January's jaw dropped. Stunned, she managed to utter, "Did you just say the electricity wasn't on yet?"

Ben nodded.

"That isn't possible. The light shining in the window is what drew my attention to the ghost in the first place!"

CHAPTER 3

As they emerged from the trees, the mansion, shrouded in wispy fingers of fog, came in to view. It appeared like a black mass against the gray sky. The thick grove of trees, that protected the estate from easy access, accentuated the effect. January shuddered. Somehow, she'd had the misplaced notion that the house would seem, somehow, less benign in the daylight, but it loomed ominously ahead of her. The closer they drew to the house, the more overwhelming the retreat idea became. How could she make this place appear less...less...malevolent?

"If there was a caretaker for the mansion, why did they let the grounds get so overgrown?" Dark junipers and thick bushes hid the windows at the front of the house.

"Money," he said flatly. "Thirty years ago, when the subsidy was set to oversee the estate, that sum was a fortune. Inflation caused this, my dear...and the caretakers drinking problem,"

She was ready and eager to see the inside of the mansion. Opening the car door, she stepped out onto the gravel driveway and drank in her first clear view of her future. She wasn't seeing the drifts of shriveled paint, cast off like a molted snakeskin caught against the rock foundation, or a sunken rose garden choked with weeds. In her mind, she saw the house with gleaming windows and bouquets of fragrant flowers lining the cement walk that would replace the overgrown dirt path that presently circled the house.

Hugging her purse to her side, she felt for the small notebook she planned to use for her notes and sketches. The depth of her determination surprised her. All she had to do was use her imagination, and the house became a beautiful residence—if only it really were that easy.

"I have a question," January said. "Wouldn't the pipes freeze without power?"

Ben nodded. "Of course it would, but it's only been off a week."

"A week?"

"My oversight entirely. The bills were sent to the old Post Office box instead of transferring to my own address. I should have let the company know."

Ben opened his door but stayed sitting in the driver's seat. "I really hope the electricity is on. If it's not...I...will not take a single step into that spooky old house."

"Oh come on!" January's voice shimmered with laughter. "I'm the one that saw the ghost, for heaven's sake. Nothing's going to hurt you." When she looked closely at him, she saw he was gripping the steering wheel so tightly that his knuckles were white from lack of blood flow and they matched the coloring of his skin around his tightly pursed lips. "OK, what gives? You look like you've seen a..." She bit the word ghost from her tongue.

"A ghost?" he said, filling in her blanks. "You must think I'm a real coward."

"I think nothing of the sort," she said. "We aren't messing around with the ordinary here, Ben. You have every reason to feel afraid, I was terrified last night. But in the daylight, I feel that there's nothing here that will hurt us. So tell me what happened to you in there?" She didn't want to humiliate him, but she was she had done just that as she watched his face pale and his eyes grow dark as a brief flash of anger pass through them.

"What makes you think I saw something in there?"

January hesitated a moment weighing her decision. She shifted her position and could feel a cold draft playing around her ankles. There were only a few people she confided in, but she wanted Ben to know about her...special ability. She took a deep breath and said, "I suppose I might as well tell you this, heaven knows you're sure to think something is the matter with me if I don't tell you this. I'm psychic."

His eyes narrowed, but he didn't take off running. "You can tell the future? Read my mind? What?"

"Ben, you don't know how close you are to my reality. I can't tell the future, but I do get pictures of things that will happen, only they aren't in context with anything in particular. I also sense things out of the range of our normal senses.

This is called clairvoyance. I am not telepathic, which means reading minds." She smiled at him shyly and said, "Lecture over."

"Whew! You know a lot about this don't you?"

"Yeah, I do," she said, smiling. "From the time I was old enough to understand, I could perceive things. Some people called it ESP, others, second sight. Whatever it was called, I hated it, most of the time."

January felt her mood grow soft and dreamy as she reminisced. "When I was seven, my friend disappeared from the school during recess. Her family feared that someone had kidnapped her, but I could hear my friend crying out to me. I ran up to a policeman and sobbed out my story. At first, he wouldn't listen, but I kept insisting until the police agreed to expand the search another two blocks. I thought it would take forever to convince the adults that Amanda was under a pile of wood. I knew she was trapped and in great danger. At dusk, they found her, cold and frightened...and she was under a woodpile one block further than the original search area... Amanda had been climbing on it when she tripped and fell. After that, I understood I was different. Until that time, I thought everyone could hear and see as I did."

Ben blinked his eyes, mesmerized. "I'm glad you're the one I'm with. Why don't you just think about the electricity and see if the lights are on?"

"Hey, you're not getting out of checking that easy. Please, tell me what happened to you in there."

"I hoped you would forget your question." Ben grumbled, then smiled at her with his lopsided grin. "I've only been in the mansion twice. The first time wasn't too bad. The house felt stuffy, oppressive, and it seemed as if someone was watching me. I could handle that, but the last time, a couple of weeks ago, was different. I was in the master bedroom fixing the window broken by the vandals." Ben hesitated, combed his fingers through his long hair, then interlocked his fingers behind his head. "I had a difficult time breathing because the smell of lilacs choked me and nearly made me sick. Then the room became icy cold. I finished as quickly as possible and got the hell out of there. I haven't been back inside since."

She opened her door again and started to step out. "I see why you're reluctant to go in there alone. I'll go with you."

"No way! You've shamed me now, lady. I'm going in by myself. If you can see a ghost and not faint, I can go open the door and flip a switch. You stay here while I see if we have light. There's no sense in you stumbling around in the fog, too," he said softly, "but if I'm not back in thirty minutes, call 911. I'll leave my phone with you."

Noticing the slight tremor in his voice as he spoke, and a quivering of his hand on the door handle, she smiled. Usually, men tried to act strong and invincible. Ben was a refreshing change from the macho-men who had come-on to her so strongly in the past. "What would your EMT friends think if they had to come and rescue you?"

Ben rolled his eyes at her and virtually jumped from the vehicle, acting as if he had to rush toward the mansion without thinking or lose his nerve. Straightening his back, he slammed the door shut with confidence and took a step toward the house. Suddenly, he stopped for a moment, then stepped back to the vehicle. As an afterthought, he reopened the door and said, "Maybe you imagined that ghost. Let's see, your psychiatrist is treating you for wild daydreams and..."

January shook her head and giggled in response at his antics. "Get real, Cottier."

"OK, OK, watch for the lights to come on. I'm out of here." He smiled at her, small lines fanned around his eyes.

It had been windy earlier, but now it was so still she could hear the crunching sound of Ben's shoes on the rocks when he rounded the vehicle. His leather jacket rode at his waist and revealed his rounded backside and muscular legs clad in tight, worn blue jeans. The muscles rippled under the soft denim and reminded her of a sleek racehorse.

Chastising herself for observing him in such a sexist manner...a mode she detested, January bit her lip and glanced at her dowdy apparel. The full denim skirt and loose cotton sweater caused her to look plump and old-fashioned, and her heavy knee socks added thickness to her slim calves. When Ben had gaped at her earlier, clad only in her robe, she had enjoyed the sensations he invoked. Now, she wished she had a pair of her old tight jeans to tantalize him into staring at her curvaceous figure so she could experience that special sexual thrill he stirred in her.

Stop it, she told herself. This was dangerous thinking. Never had she thought this way about a man. She was familiar with running from, not instigating the chase.

January returned her thoughts to Ben and his chore. The fog had lifted, and she watched him take out a set of keys from his pocket and momentarily, the heavy door swung open. Even though it was morning, the sky was dark and filled with moisture-filled clouds so low she felt she could reach up and touch them. The trill of a Meadowlark split the gloom. The outside lights flickered beside the front door, and then yellow light sparkled in the small panes in the door.

The light made the house look so much more inviting. Ben stepped out on the porch. "Come on in," he hollered to her.

January enthusiastically tossed open the door and raced across the gravel and skipped up the steps.

"Well, here it is." He widened the opening for her as she walked past him. "I'll give you the grand tour."

"Wow," she uttered, at a loss for a better word. Turning a full circle, she looked at the foyer that was decidedly more like a large room rather than an entryway. It was grand, to say the least with hand-painted ceiling panels, dark oak woodwork, and a huge chandelier hung in the middle of the room. Digging into her purse, she pulled out her notebook and started writing. "I'll move that desk right here, for a reception area." She walked further into the entryway. And put a…"

Abruptly, she stopped as she caught sight of the drawing room. She stood in the doorway, mesmerized by the beauty. Even covered with dust, the room was exquisite.

"You like it?" Ben asked.

January nodded. She knew this room. The rug on the floor took her attention. It was Persian and ancient. Would she have this familiar feeling as she walked through the whole house? "Could you, would you tell me something?" The words stuck in her throat.

Ben took her hand and guided her into the room. Lines of concern etched the skin between his eyes. "Sure. What is it? You look worried."

His hand felt warm and comforting in hers. "Tell me, through that door, is there a library with stained glass windows and a fireplace both trimmed with marble?"

Ben nodded.

"And are all the books safely displayed behind glass doors?"

He eyed her quizzically. "Uh, yeah. How did you know that? Did you see it yesterday when you were looking for me?"

She turned away from him, sauntering toward the door leading into the dining room. "No," she said, shaking her head as she pushed the door open. "This room is on the other side of the mansion from where I was. I feel as if I've seen this room before. It's the oddest sensation."

"Déjà-vu?" He whispered, leaning back against the fireplace, he stretched his arm across the marble mantle and looked at her thoughtfully. "You're really scaring me. First, the tale of spotting a ghost and now, your psychic sensitivity to this house, I don't think I can stand much more of this."

She returned her attention to him, her eyes seeking his. She needed understanding; someone to give her strength, but she could read by the lines of tension drawn across his face that he was just as frightened as she.

"I'm sorry to upset you, Ben, but this is the way I feel. Can't you see I have to find out everything I can about this mansion, its history, and secrets? I want this house, it's...important to me in some strange way, a way I don't understand."

"I still think you should sell it."

She thrust out her chin defiantly. "And I think your idea is out of the question."

"Can't blame a guy for trying." He walked toward where she stood in the middle of the room and firmly grasped her arms. "Let's see the rest of this house. You will protect me, won't you?" He smiled at her, easing the tension with his light, joking question.

Laughing, she slid her arm through his. "Come on. We'll protect each other."

He showed her through the house like a tour guide in a museum. And the tour went on and on, through the dusty library that gave her shudders, into a large kitchen, then up the back stairs that led to the second floor. At the top of the stairs, January stopped and looked down the wide hallway. "Gosh! How many bedrooms are up here?"

"There are twelve."

"I suppose that's good since this will be a writer's retreat."

"Maybe you should see the bedrooms before you decide to use them all. Some are very plain. Nothing that would interest a guest. The larger rooms are on this floor. The servant quarters are on the third floor behind the ballroom. Those rooms are smaller, but each has its own bathroom."

January was delighted with what she had seen so far. This house was everything she had ever dreamed of. It reminded her of a middle-age woman who had spent all life raising her family. She was a faded beauty, not from neglect, but from lack of priorities. January would remedy this problem with the house in short order.

"I haven't seen the ghost..."

"...Yet," January interrupted. "Oh," she said, "I'm sorry. That's a bad habit of mine. My father scolded me about interrupting. I guess it's a hard lesson to learn." The mention of her father reminded her of why she was here...the adoption, the inheritance, and her driving compulsion to find the person behind all of this. She was grateful and inquisitive.

January's feet began to throb as they neared the last bedroom on the second floor. She had insisted on entering each room. "I'm surprised at the condition of the house. I thought it would be run-down, needing major repairs. This place could be ready to go with a thorough cleaning."

Reaching for the doorknob, Ben turned and looked at her. "Don't be so hasty. There're always setbacks when dealing with old houses. I know, I'm the realtor, remember?"

She smiled softly, enjoying Ben's light mood. She wished he'd remain this way. She couldn't figure him out. One moment, he seems withdrawn and the next, jovial.

They were entering the bedroom when her vision blurred, and a buzzing sound from deep in her head began to grow stronger; it ebbed and flowed like an ocean of distant voices sobbing and crying Jannnuarrry...Jannnuarrry. The room called to her, pulling at her. Finally, she stepped into the room.

Her sight cleared, and then the voices diminished as a feeling of peace filled her heart. After all the months of emotional turmoil, she felt, here in this room, that she had, finally, returned home. She was keeping this room for herself. Suddenly Ben looked ill and he didn't need to hear about her psychic ideas.

January looked deeply into his eyes. There was a glazed look about them. She bit down on her lips to suppress her smile. How was she going to break it to him? He was psychically sensitive, too.

"Ben, come on you need to sit down." She drew him to the window seat and guided him to sit. The room was beautiful. A canopy bed graced one wall. The deep-burgundy, floral coverlet reflected the elegance of another time. The window seat cushions and wing chair material matched the bed. She touched the cloth. It felt heavy and durable. "It still looks like new." January ambled through the room, jotting an inventory in her little book: An oriental rug, dusty baskets, and original oil paintings caught her eye.

Another marble-faced fireplace dominated the wall across from the bed. Floor to ceiling windows stood beside the hearth. A door leading to the balcony nestled in the window area was camouflaged so well, that if January hadn't seen the glittering of a cut-glass doorknob, she might have missed it altogether. She brushed back the draperies. "Oh, look. All the windows are topped by half-moon shaped stained glass. Why would they cover this beautiful accent?"

Ben shook his head to remove the fog. "I don't know why you want to keep this house. It's an old, spooky mausoleum."

"Where does this door lead?" she asked aloud as she walked across the room and tossed open the door. "Oh, Ben, this is exquisite. Look at the bathroom," she cried and entered the room. All surfaces of the room were clad with white marble. A burgundy veining added depth and color. The effect was nearly blinding. Once cleaned, the luster would be dramatic. The urge to clean and polish was strong.

A gigantic claw-foot bathtub, more extensive than any she had ever seen, dominated one wall. January touched the elaborate gold fixtures and imagined herself stretching out in the oversized tub with thick bubbles tickling her nose. At that moment she knew this was her room.

January heard Ben pacing nervously from the bed to the bedroom door and back again, eager to leave the room. January re-entered the bedroom, touching the heavy fabric on the wing chair, studying the excellent quality. Who were the people that had decorated this house so lovingly years ago? She wondered. "Is there a newspaper in this community? I want to investigate the Call family; really find out who they were."

Dropping, once again on to the cushions of the window seat, Ben put his head in his hands. "What's happening to me, Jan?" She sat down near him and put her arm around his shoulders. She couldn't tell him. Instinctively, she knew he wasn't ready. "I know it's strange and frightening, but we have to find out what is going on around here. The ghost hasn't hurt either of us, so I figure we're relatively safe while in the house."

The words were barely out of her mouth when the room turned icy cold. "I feel her presence in here. Can you?" January asked him.

Ben nodded. "But I don't feel so afraid with you here."

"Thanks for your vote of confidence. Let's go about our business and let Calico join us if she wants to." Putting the apprehension from her mind, she looked around assessing the amount of work needed to revitalize the bedroom. The hardwood floors needed refinishing. The fabric looked sturdy enough for cleaning. "I'm going to move into the house, this room in particular, as soon as possible."

Ben ran his fingers through his hair, combing it back out of his eyes. It was thick and heavy and had a tendency to fall over his forehead. Walking across the room, he switched off the bathroom light. "Jan, why did you call her Calico?"

January stood and walked to the bedroom door before answering. She wasn't sure of the answer herself until she blurted out, "Because of the blue calico dress she's wearing. I have to call her something besides *ghost*. That's not very becoming."

"You haven't seen the attic or the basement," Ben said, changing the subject.

"Ugh, I don't want to, either. My feet hurt. Let's go back downstairs." As she left the room, she looked back over her shoulder and felt her heart tug at the thought of leaving. This was love at first sight, and she could hardly wait to return.

"You have to see the ballroom. Surely, your feet can handle just a little more abuse. It's the most impressive part of the house," he said and drew her out of the room. They walked back down the hallway to the wide staircase in the middle of the house. A brass stair rod at the back of each step held the vibrant red carpet runner in place.

January touched the polished banister lightly as she lingered at the landing before ascending the last flight of steps to the third floor. "Do you think my idea has any merit?"

Ben sighed. "Jan, I hate to admit this, but yes, I think you could make this work. I just can't imagine how you are going to do it."

As they reached the last step, January saw the beautiful ballroom. She walked into the middle of the room staring at the ceiling that was a series of spiked Georgia pine ceiling beams that rose to a dramatic height. Between the joists, windows filled the gap. At one end, a musician's loft dropped down from the ceiling. Tiffany-style chandeliers with a verdigris finish reflected in the gloss finish of the maple floor. She turned in circles to drink in the splendor, and it took her breath away.

"Look at these bench cushions! Is this where people sat waiting to dance?" She fingered the blood-red velvet where strands of some undetermined stuffing poked out. "This fill is very strange. What is this?"

"Horsehair."

She snapped her hand back. "Horsehair! Maybe I won't have them recovered, just duplicated with clean foam cushions." January fell silent for a moment as she gazed about the huge room. "You know, this would be a perfect conference room. I could hire a famous author to present workshops for the in-house writers."

"Hmmm...that's a great idea. Let's look at the rest of the floor. The servants' rooms are back here." The couple wound their way through stacked furniture to peer into the rooms. "The intercom system, laundry chute, and dumbwaiter run all the way up here. So does the elevator."

"What?" January cried. You've had me climbing all these stairs when I didn't have to?"

"Now, wait a minute. I thought you needed to see this house how it was designed. The elevator was added by the family a long time ago, but it still works."

January nodded her head thoughtfully. "I hadn't thought about it, but I'd imagine that to be compliant with the Disabilities Act, I would need this necessary amenity. And I can advertise this feature. Who knows? It might bring me a lot more business."

"There's also a fire suppression system throughout the entire house and fire hoses on each floor. That should help you meet fire codes."

January shook her head in wonder. "This house was way ahead of its time. Lucky for me."

"I'll show you the basement another time. It's in the same condition as this wing, furniture piled everywhere."

"What's down there?"

They started down the steps. "The laundry room, of course, you saw that yesterday. The motor for the ancient vacuum cleaner."

"Vacuum cleaner?"

"Uh huh, the pipes run in all the walls. I can't imagine how they had enough power to clean anything, but it's there. There's also a vault, furnace room and boilers for the heating system, and the chauffeur's bedroom."

"You look tired," January said. "Did you get in late after your ambulance call last night?" she asked.

"Midnight, maybe. I stopped by the Lounge for a beer to unwind."

"I know you can't discuss it, but if you do need anyone to talk to, remember, I'm a nurse." Reaching into her purse, she retrieved his pager and handed it to him. "I forgot that I put it in my purse. I was afraid you'd get a call and couldn't hear your page."

He smiled faintly. "I'm impressed. Most civilians don't understand the importance of the ambulance service. Thanks. If you joined the rescue service, I could talk to you about everything that happens."

His words made her smile. "I don't know, Ben. Let's see how this goes, but I might be interested. How is the patient you helped last night?"

"I can tell you this much. It was an automobile accident about three miles east of town. I don't know if the guy will pull through or not. He's about my age, has two young children."

She reached out and firmly gripped his upper arm with a squeeze of compassion and emotional support. He looked so sad. Being a volunteer EMT was an emotionally draining profession. "I'm sorry. Thank God, there are people like you, willing to help others. I've worked in emergency rooms enough to know that the EMT's on the front line really do save lives and make our work a little easier. At least we have a patient to work with."

"I'm the lucky one," he offered. "My work allows me time to drop everything and go. I couldn't do that if I were tied down to a classroom or a desk."

"I never thought of that. Small towns are different than cities where the paramedics and firemen are paid positions." He looked into her eyes then brought his lips to hers. A crazy spinning started behind her eyes, and she came alive, every cell in her body ready to accept the sensations he was invoking. The kiss was more intoxicating than brandy, hotter than a Habanero pepper and more unique than anything she had allowed herself to enjoy. Wrapping his arms around her, he smashed her against his yearning body, and they fit perfectly. He knew at once that she was the last piece on a huge puzzle board.

Finally, he broke the kiss and pushed his hair from his forehead.

"I like your hair," she said. "And the way sun glitters against the white." She reached up and touched a silver-shot curl and felt her face flush.

"Audra hates my hair this way. If she had her way, it would be cut short and slicked back like business tycoons wore theirs in the roaring twenties."

January's heart fluttered to her toes, and she took an involuntary step away from Ben. Audra? Who was she? The easy way he spoke of the woman indicated that he must be involved. Darn, this bad luck. Maybe the magazine articles were right, there weren't enough men to go around.

She smiled at him, but her heart felt heavy with disappointment. The thick fog surrounded them as they walked shoulder-to-shoulder down the driveway. The physical magnetism between them remained a robust force. *Could he feel it too, or was he so taken by this faceless Audra that he was unaware of their mystical passion that transcended into another dimension?*

CHAPTER 4

"You could have left me a note telling me she was coming." Ben leaned back against the edge of his desk and leveled his fiery glare at his father. He crossed his boot-clad ankles and stuffed his hands into the pockets of his faded jeans. His head ached as the blood pounded in his temples. Damn, he was angry. If his father kept interloping in the business, Ben thought he might find himself needing blood pressure pills from the stress.

Running a successful real estate business was all he had ever wanted to do. Ben started working at the office when he was in high school and worked each summer during his college days. But Ben couldn't remember a sale his father hadn't meddled in and it caused Ben to assume that his dad thought he didn't know what he was doing.

Bennett Cottier sat in the leather chair facing his son. He narrowed his eyes and uttered sourly, "Stop talking down to me. I want to know what you have done to get rid of that woman?"

Ben sighed and shook his head in response. His father wasn't going to like it, but Ben wanted to keep January in his life, not send her back to Denver. "I've done nothing, nothing at all." He said, shaking his head slightly.

"She couldn't possibly want that mansion. She'll take one look at it and be thankful she accepted the money. When is your ranch sale final?"

"We're supposed to close in two weeks, but I haven't heard from them in a few days."

"Sit down! You make me nervous." The older man cut in. He crossed his leg over the top of his slim thigh and leaned toward Ben. Bennett had recently returned from a golfing trip to Arizona, and when he frowned, the deeply tanned skin between his eyes became deeply creased. He was in his mid-sixties, but his thick white hair, prematurely grayed, and trim body made him appear much younger.

"Suit yourself," Ben sighed. He walked around the large desk and dropped into the chair causing a familiar squawk to emit from the springs. It sounded somewhat like a balloon being tied off and it broke the silence in the room. Ben leaned back in the chair and laced his fingers over his chest.

His dad looked uncomfortable sitting in the worn leather chair and not at the helm of the company behind this old desk; the notion caused a plummeting sensation in the pit of his stomach. Ben wondered why he had given the reins to him in the first place if he wasn't going to retire and let Ben operate the business. "Miss Mohr... she's keeping the mansion; I just returned from showing it to her, she plans to operate it as a writer's retreat."

"How could you let this happen?" Bennett sputtered.

Ben observed his father looking accusingly at him. The expression on his face didn't change much, but the skin around his mouth paled then was replaced by a glowing red. He had seen this look more times than he wanted to remember.

In high school, Ben had been an outstanding student. He excelled in basketball, but he loved all the sports that were offered in the small school. Sports activities were the primary weekend interest of the whole community. After being a hometown star, his college years were more sedate until he discovered—women.

His social life became much more important than his studies, and that's when his father had developed "the look." And it worked, too. After a call from Ben's adviser, Bennett made a special trip to the University of Wyoming campus. From that time forward, Ben's love life continued, but not to the extent it damaged his grades.

"This could directly impact the sale of your ranch. You know that the Willis Corporation is expecting to buy the house, too. There isn't another home in this area that's as large and exquisite as Pine Gables. Where do you expect them to house their top executives when they are in the area?"

Bennett's words dropped Ben back into the conversation. "Hey, don't blame me," Ben sarcastically countered snapping the chair upright. "If you'd told me about the phone call, I could've called and possibly discouraged her coming here in the first place."

Here we go again! The words raged in Ben's mind. Wouldn't dad ever let up? Dealing with his father fatigued and irritated him. Speaking to January Mohr's lawyer without telling him was a classic example of the man's interference.

Bennett straightened his back at his son's accusation. "Don't get testy with me, boy. If this were my sale, the papers would be signed by this time and..."

"... and it's not your sale and, in fact, you have nothing to do with it, it's mine, and I'll do it my way."

"Your way? Botched up, that's your way! You'll end up losing the business. Why the estate has been settled for over four months. You should have just offered her money and let that doofus of an attorney hand her an envelope full of bills instead of the deed! Get that girl out of town and sell the estate. That's the way to run a business."

Ben knotted his hands into a fist at his side, but he wasn't about to let his face express his emotions. That would be a sure way to show his father that the older, more experienced man had won.

"No!"

"What did you say to me?"

"I told you...no." Ben's voice sounded calm and matter-of-fact, but inside, he seethed. His father was a tough man to defy.

Bennett stood, then marched proudly to the door and said, "Bring Audra over for drinks tonight, and you can tell me how you got rid of that mousy woman."

"And just what makes you think January Mohr is mousy?"

"You know Livingston, and I are friends. He happened to mention, once, that his client was rather, dowdy."

"Don't make up your mind until you meet her, dad. From what I've seen, she's a wonderful woman."

"But not a looker like Audra, I bet." The older man winked at his son.

Slowly, Ben walked to the front door behind his father. He wanted to tell him to go straight to hell and to mind his own business, but he couldn't and wouldn't do that. This was his father, after all. It would serve no purpose to rile the old man.

"Well, I might as well tell you, you're going to hear it somewhere. Audra and I called off our engagement; we're not right for each other," he stammered and then opened the door for his father.

Bennett's eyes softened as he looked at him. "I hate to hear that, son. Audra's a wonderful girl. She'd make you a fine wife; do a lot for your career, too." he said softly and with sincerity. Turning, he started down the concrete steps.

Ben hesitated as his father walked toward the vehicle, then he rushed down the steps to follow him. This was a golden opportunity to play matchmaker. "Dad," he called and rushed up to his father's side. "She's not for me, but she would be perfect for you."

The older man spun around and faced Ben; his mouth twitched as if he was trying very hard to suppress a grin. "I don't know, Ben. Do you really think so?" he asked, and his eyebrows rose in question. He quickly averted his eyes, but not before Ben caught a glittering twinkle of excitement as he turned away.

Ben nodded slowly. "Think about it. She would be a good hostess for your parties; she likes your lifestyle. Mine would bore her silly in only a few months."

"That's an interesting theory, son, and I will think about this." Bennett walked toward his sleek car, waved and ducked inside. Before driving away, he lowered the window and asked, "Do you really think Audra would be interested in me?"

Ben placed his hands above the window of the car and leaned down, speaking his mind. "Yes, I do. If she had her way, she'd have made me over into your image. She's wanted someone like you all along, not me."

"Well, no matter what happens, I'm sorry," Bennett said.

"Don't worry about it. Get going, now." He slapped the roof of the car in dismissal and walked back to the office.

Ben flopped into chair kicked his feet up on the desk and locked his fingers behind his head. Every time his father visited, he felt exhausted and depressed; he had no energy and felt like he could sleep the rest of the day. He rubbed his temples with his fingertips to ease the throbbing pain that radiated from his tight shoulder muscles to the top of his head.

He had to finalize the sale of his ranch and try to convince January to sell the mansion. This would be the biggest sale he had orchestrated, and it would prove to his father, conclusively, that he was perceptive in business. So far, he had kept his father out of the Call contracts; a problematic assignment, indeed.

Ben knew that he had proved himself quite capable of running The Cottier Agency. He was thirty-two-years-old, he had operated the real estate office since he graduated from college and he had increased the profits immeasurably over the years.

Now, Ben's concern was January Mohr. He would make sure got her share of the money and that she was treated fairly. It was important to him to show his father that hurting other people just to get ahead wasn't necessary. Once he sold the entire Call estate, including Pine Gables, Ben expected his father would be more at ease with his retirement and Ben's capabilities, leave the area and let him handle the business.

The only thing wrong with the picture Ben was painting in his mind was the nagging feeling that he would be selling himself, heart and soul, for money.

"CATHY, COME AND HELP me move the sofa, please." January's breath whistled in and out from the exertion of trying to push the heavy piece across the parlor.

She plunked down on the sheet-covered arm, then fell over backward onto the cushions and stared at the freshly painted walls. She had only been in Garrison for two weeks, but the house was really shaping up. She had cleaned and painted most of the first floor.

Moments later, January heard Jim and Cathy enter the back hallway. Their voices grew louder as they approached from the foyer. She began to rise from the sofa, but Cathy's words froze her in place.

"I can't get anything done! First, she wants me to wash curtains, then all the dishes in this house! I despise her, I really do, Jim," Cathy whined to her husband. "Can't she do anything herself?"

The malicious tone of Cathy's voice startled January, and she couldn't move from her secluded spot. What had she done to Cathy? After all, she had let the couple stay on, Jim as caretaker and Cathy as a housekeeper. They lived on the property rent-free, and she arranged a decent wage for them besides. She needed them now, and when the retreat opened, she would need them even more. January thought she was becoming friends with Cathy, but from the vindictive tone in Cathy's words, apparently, she was mistaken.

Jim's voice faded as he turned. "Now, Hon, she's doin' a lot, too," Jim said in a placating manner. "She'll find you when she needs you. Come on."

After the sounds of their footsteps faded, January sat up. She'd never heard anyone speaking about her with such venom. A feeling of dread churned in the pit of her stomach. She'd always thought there was something strange about Cathy; and now, her internal vibrations kicked into high gear, warning her about the woman. Over the years, January had learned not to ignore those feelings, and she planned to watch Cathy very closely.

January stopped in her tracks. Usually, she didn't pick up feelings that were related to herself personally, and this confused her. Why was this happening now?

Suddenly, the faint smell of lilacs filtered through the room and the room temperature began to drop. "Calico, I know you're there. I can smell the flowers. Do you like the work we've done on the house?" The entity didn't appear, but January felt a peaceful sensation course through her body. She assumed that was the way Calico felt, too. January took a deep breath and exhaled slowly to center herself to try and absorb more feelings emanating from the ghost, but she was too late, the room had returned to normal. Calico was gone.

January strode through the formal dining room leading to an enormous kitchen and found Cathy with her hands in the sink. The long counter was covered with dish towels and crystal stemware drying on them.

January stood in the doorway watching her. Cathy was tall and thin. She wore her brown hair pulled back from her face and secured with an elastic band at the nape of her neck. Her movements were jerky, revealing the anger she felt. Why? January thought to herself.

"Cathy?"

The woman jumped. "Oh! You scared me!" Soapsuds dripped from her hands onto the tiled floor. Her smile, a mere tightening of her lips, never reached her eyes. "What do you want?"

Yeah, sure, like you didn't know, January thought to herself and then she spoke aloud. "I need help moving the furniture because the floor finishers will be here shortly. I want them to sand the wood floors in these rooms today. They said that they could do it if we had the larger items moved before they got here."

"Well, Jim's outside. Why don't you ask him to help you?" Cathy said sarcastically as she turned back to the sink. "I'm busy."

January fought to keep her temper. "Jim's clearing the brush around the house. This won't take long, and the dishes will keep. I need your help." She spun on her heel and stomped out to the room. "Now!"

"OK! OK! You don't have to get so snippy."

January gritted her teeth. What was wrong with Cathy, PMS?

Cathy followed January into the drawing room. "So when do we have to move all this crap back, as soon as I start doing the glasses again?" Cathy sniveled, grunting with exertion as she hefted her side of the couch, nearly toppling January in the process.

"No. We don't have to do that. The finishers will replace the furniture," January said as she planted her feet and lifted the weight. Cathy wasn't going to intimidate her.

Chimes pealed through the first floor of the mansion. January and Cathy looked at each other in surprise. "Wow!" January said, her mouth formed a perfect circle. "Apparently Jim got the doorbell fixed."

"I'll bet you can hear that bell clean up to the attic," Cathy said with disbelief.

"Did you think it would sound so Gothic?" January's breath caught in her chest.

They set the couch down, and January went to answer the door. She opened it to find Ben standing on the porch.

January's heart jumped in her chest. He hadn't been back since he showed her the mansion nearly two weeks ago. She had talked to him on the telephone a few times, but he was always too busy to come to the house. "Well, stranger what brings you here?"

"I came to help you."

"You want to help me? Why?"

"This project sounds like fun, and I want to see how this museum turns into something...nice." He was dressed in faded jeans with holes at the knees, and a light blue work shirt with the sleeves rolled up to his elbows.

"The only time I've talked to you is when I called. And each time you brought up the notion that I should have you sell the house. I still refuse to consider it."

Ben leaned back against the porch railing and looked down at her. His boyish smile was in complete contrast to the silver in his hair. "Whew, you're a tough number. I admit it, I'm guilty as charged. But I also wanted to see how you're getting on with the project. And I am here to help you."

January smiled, opened the door wider and gestured for him to enter. How could she turn him down when he looked so sexy and so darned sincere? "All right then, come on inside and see for yourself how we're doing."

He softly whistled as he stepped through the threshold. "Whew, you have been busy. It even feels better in here."

She looked up at him. "What does that mean?" she asked gently, wondering what he was sensing. She still felt Ben was sensitive to psychic impressions. He almost seemed afraid of the house.

"The quality of workmanship in the house still amazes me. It's sure not taking you very long to overhaul it."

January shrugged. "The second floor is another matter. All the wood floors are dull and covered with millions of scratches. At least some thoughtful person spared the exquisite pieces of furniture in the attic and basement by spreading sheets over them."

"Is there anything you can use hidden under there?" Ben walked over to the sofa that was sitting in the middle of the room where she and Cathy had left it. He sat down on the dusty cover.

"Oh, yes! Antique bedroom furniture, beautiful oil paintings, there's just too much to remember."

"Where's Cathy?"

"I don't know." January looked around the room. "She was here with me when I went to answer the door."

"How did you fill these rooms with so much sunshine?"

January snuggled into the corner of the sofa and folded her arms across her breast. "You're responsible for the change, you know."

A momentary flash of surprise crossed his face, then, as quickly as it had come, it was gone, and he frowned with confusion.

"You gave me Jim and Cathy. They've been so much help. Jim's cutting the old, overgrown Juniper bushes away from the windows. Cathy has worked really hard to get the windows washed. Now, light can flood into the rooms, and I think everything looks beautiful."

"That's all you've done?"

"We've painted the walls and ceilings. And we've washed everything. You'd be surprised how many layers of dirt we've removed."

Ben smiled. "I guess you won't be needing my help then."

"Not so fast," January said, glancing at the ceiling. "We have the master bedroom and the main floor to finish, so I won't turn down your help."

Cathy entered the room with a tray of coffee and cookies. "Hello, Ben. I thought you two would like some snacks. It's such a pleasure to see you. Isn't it just wonderful what January has done with the house?"

January wondered what Cathy was up to. After the sickeningly sweet pretense, it made January want to throw up. Instead, she smiled and gestured toward the dining room. "Just leave the things on the table, and we'll help ourselves." She tried to make her voice sound sincere, but Ben gave her a questioning look.

They watched Cathy walk from the room, through the foyer, and into the dining room. Even at that distance, they heard her set the tray on the table with more force than was necessary and stomp out.

"What was that all about?"

Oh, nothing," she said, scuffing her shoe over a deep scratch on the floor.

"What's going on? he asked softly.

His peaceful manner brought a torrent of words. January told him what she'd overheard.

Ben was quiet and listened to her with a troubled expression. "As far as I'm concerned, I'll tell them to pack their things and go."

He started to stand, and January pulled on his arm. "No, d-don't do that! They have helped me a lot. I don't know what's the matter with Cathy, but this is the first time she's acted this way. Firing them is just too radical. Maybe Cathy's having a bad day. Besides, it's my place to fire them, not yours!"

Ben raised his eyebrows and took a deep breath. "So you want to give them another chance?"

January nodded her answer unable to speak for pushing her tears back. "It's not them, it's her." God! This was a mess.

"All right then, let's get busy." He reached out and grasped her hands, pulling her up from the sofa as he stood. "Hey, I've got a question for you first. Why's this couch in the middle of the room?"

January laughed and explained to him about the floor refinishing.

"Didn't you get a little ahead of yourself?"

Her eyebrows knit together. "What do you mean?"

"Y'know, those huge sanders will throw dust all over the house. I think you should have done the floors first."

Indignation flooded through her. She had worried about that, too, but she wasn't going to admit it to Ben. "The company representative told me that dust would be no problem because the new machines have a vacuuming system, but..."

"... Hey! I was just trying to help."

"Trying to make me seem dull-witted," she said under her breath as she walked from the room.

"What?"

"Oh, nothing. Let's get that coffee before it gets cold." They walked to the dining room to find Cathy, in her snit, had spilled the dark brown liquid across the napkins and onto some of the cookies.

Ben raised his eyebrows. "Where's your paper towels?"

"In the kitchen."

He touched her shoulders and led her to a heavy wooden chair. "See if you can salvage a cookie for me and I'll go get something to clean up this mess. By the way, I don't like pre-dunked cookies."

January smiled feeling a warm sensation spread through her body. It must have taken a lot of courage for Ben to come here. She felt unusually happy that he wanted to be here and to help her.

After Ben returned with a thick wad of towels, they set at the table drinking coffee. "What's your plan for today? he asked.

"I'm taking down the drapes in this room," she said. "They might be considered elegant, but I don't like green, and besides that, they don't allow any light into the room. I didn't want to strip this elegant wallpaper, so I needed all the light I get in here."

Ben turned in his chair and looked out into the foyer and into the drawing room. "You've changed the place so much, I totally missed the lack of window coverings in the other rooms."

January nodded. "And there won't be for a while. I want embroidered white sheers down here. They should diffuse the light nicely."

"Is there a problem?" Ben frowned and then studied January's face.

"The windows are such strange sizes that I can't buy them ready-made. I don't know anyone around here that can do this."

"Well, I do. Where's your phone?"

"What, no cellular?" January joked.

"Nope. The weather was too nice today, for work, so I left my phone at the office."

She pointed to the foyer where the phone rested on the desk. She stood and raised her arms above her head and looked at the drapes while she stretched. The ceilings were high and her ladder tall. She didn't like heights.

Moments later, Ben walked into the dining room. "Problem solved."

January was on the top rung of the ladder.

"What did you..." She stretched to reach the last hook in the drapery heading, and the ladder began to tip with her unbalanced weight.

"January, be careful...don't..." Ben ran toward the window.

January felt herself falling, and her throat tightened into a scream. Suddenly, she was floating in mid-air. The ladder righted itself, and she drifted back toward it.

Ben reached her side as she was regaining her balance. "How did you do that?" she gasped out of breath from the sheer terror of the near accident.

Ben shook his head. "I didn't do anything. I saw you start to fall and rushed over here. That was the strangest thing. I thought you were completely off the step when the ladder straightened up. Then you seemed to hover in the air for a second." His face was white and his dark huge.

"But...but...if felt as if you caught me in mid-air. If it wasn't you, then it had to be Calico."

"Calico?"

"Uh-huh," She nodded her head. "You know...my ghost."

"Oh, come on, January. Do you expect me to believe that?"

"Do you have another explanation for what just happened? I was floating in the air for heaven's sake!"

Ben gulped, then said, "I-I...just don't want to believe it was r-real!"

January forgot her jitters as she scrambled off the ladder. She rushed to Ben's side and led him back into the drawing room, setting him down on the sofa. He looked so pale. This had really shaken him up.

She instinctively drew him into her embrace to comfort him, and his arms went around her of their own volition. He looked into her green eyes and slowly leaned toward her, his lips grazed hers in a soft kiss.

She relaxed, feeling as if she were soaring again above the ladder and she parted her lips.

Ben touched her bottom lip with his sweet tasting tongue which sent January's mind whirling. He was so masculine smelling like the pine trees that surrounded the estate. She felt like she was melting into his body, becoming one, fused with the kiss.

Ever so slowly, she pulled away from the spiraling whirlwind of emotion and stood. "We can't do this. How are you going to explain this to Audra?"

Ben straightened his shoulders and tipped his head as he looked at her. "Audra? How do you know about her?"

She shook her head as if to clear the last of the dulling fog caused by the kiss. "When you were here before y-you mentioned her."

"Oh." He hesitated for a moment. "There is a lot you don't know about that relationship."

"You don't have to explain. We just won't kiss ever again."

"Oh yes, we will." Ben brought both of his hands to her face and pulled her lips against his. His kiss deepened, and he slid his hands down her arms, then pushed her away from him. "I was engaged to Audra Lowrey until a month ago when we realized we just weren't suited for each other."

January's heart lurched with elation. It seemed as if the room became more focused, the light from the windows brighter and she realized she was starting to fall in love with Ben Cottier.

She couldn't think of this, it was too overwhelming, too soon...too stupid! January asked, "Do you want to see what we have done to the bedrooms?" She groaned inside. Why had she said that?

His sharply arched brow rose to a sharp point. "Sure. But first, let me tell you about the window coverings."

"Oh! I'd forgotten all about that with all this excitement." What she didn't say was his kiss stirred her and wiped away all practical thoughts from her mind.

"Mrs. Beemer has an in-home business. She sews just about anything you want. She has books of fabrics to choose from. I left her number on your desk by the telephone."

"Small towns?" January asked. She took a baked cookie from the tray. "Do you want coffee?"

Ben nodded. "Just black, please. I've learned quite a bit about home decorating being in the real estate business. The owners have an easier time selling their houses if the homes are in good condition. Y'know, carpet cleaned, fresh paint on the outside and of course, color-coordinated draperies." He smiled, but his eyes were somehow different. They were filled with lust.

"I'm grateful you knew about this," she said sincerely as she bit into the cookie and chewed thoughtfully. She swallowed then looked over at him and said, "I'm sorry for the way I reacted when you told me about the dust from the floor finishing. I would hate to have everything ruined. Can you imagine Cathy's reaction if I'd asked her to re-wash the windows?" she laughed and poured him more coffee from the antique silver service she had found in the basement.

As he reached for the cup, she studied his hands. They were sturdy, callused and very tan, not like the hands of someone that sat at a desk most of the time. The idea that Ben had psychic ability intrigued her. What would happen if they both reached out to the ghost, would it materialize? The biggest question remained—would Ben explore this side?

"From what you've told me, I wouldn't have the courage to ask her," he whispered and looked over his shoulder in an exaggerated manner, as if he was frightened Cathy would hear him. He smiled at his joke.

January's face turned red as she started to laugh and she covered her mouth, afraid she'd choke on the sip of coffee she'd taken. "Quit fooling around. What if she overhears you? If you want to see the results of hard work and the second story, you had better finish your coffee. After all the cleaning we've done, you aren't going to take it with you.

"Yes, Ma'am," he said jovially.

The kiss lay soft and warm between them, but it had added a nervous edge to their conversation. Hopefully, he would stop trying to get her to sell the mansion. She couldn't, not when the house was just beginning to take shape.

"Lead the way," Ben said as he placed the delicate coffee cup and its saucer on the table.

He dropped his arm over her thin shoulder as they walked toward the staircases in the foyer that lead to the upper floors. Suddenly, Ben froze. "Do you feel that?" The atmosphere in the house had changed. The air felt heavy and sharply cold. "I feel like pins are sticking me in the back of my neck!"

"I-I feel it, too," she whispered.

"What is it?"

"Calico."

"Your ghost? Why didn't I feel like this a while ago when you were floating in mid-air?"

"I don't know," she whispered, "maybe we were in a state of shock."

He hugged January to his side and took a deep breath. "OK, Calico or whatever your name is. We know you're here. What do you want?"

The charged air seemed to gather at the head of the stairs leaving in its wake a feeling of friction.

"Think about her, Ben. Help me. I want to see her." Ben took a deep breath and shuddered. "How?"

"Close your eyes and release the tension in your body."

She looked up at him as his eyes slammed shut and she felt the grip of his hand weaken. She looked at the head of the stairs where a collection of vapor was taking shape. All the sounds in the room seemed to amplify. The ticking of the grandfather clock that stood poised against the drawing room wall and the creaking of the house itself roared in her ears. "Calico," she murmured incredulously.

Ben's eyes flew open.

The apparition, wispy and faint, looked like an elderly woman.

Ben squeezed January tighter and whispered, "She's just as you described." January pulled from his grasp and stepped toward the staircase.

"What are you doing?" Ben cried and tried to hold her back.

"She's beckoning us to follow her. I want to see where she leads." January rushed up the stairs with Ben close behind her. They followed her down the hallway. When they reached the master bedroom, she seemed to walk through the closed door.

Ben turned his head and looked directly at January. His face was quite pale. January opened the door and entered the room. The smell of lilacs was overwhelming, like a solid wall of fragrance.

Ben followed behind her. Suddenly, he gasped. "That's it! That's the smell I remember!" Calico stood in the corner of the room near a cherry dressing table.

Slowly, January eased her way toward the ghost and asked, "What are you trying to tell us? Is there something in this room we need to know about?" She was close enough to the specter to see the yellow flowers on the blue calico dress. Lace-edged the collar and cuffs. From her neck hung a golden locket in the shape of a heart. Calico stroked the pendant.

"Show me...show me," January implored as she drew nearer.

Gradually, Calico began to fade.

"Wait..." January cried as she rushed to the spot where the ghost had stood only seconds before. Tears streamed down her face. "What are you trying to show me? Please, come back!"

Ben rushed to her. "Easy honey, she'll come back." He gathered her in his arms.

January felt so foolish allowing him to see her cry, but there was no controlling her emotions. The tears and sobs escaped in a rush. Calico was trying to show something to her. She felt it deep within her.

"Ben, I want to get this room finished so I can move into the house."

He shook his head in disbelief and wiped a tear from her cheek. "I don't think that's a good idea. Look how upset you are.

"But I have to know. I think this has something to do with my adoption. I can't stand not knowing who my natural parents are. I have to know why they gave me away. I know you can't understand how I feel but..."

"Don't feel so sure about that," he broke in. "I'm adopted, too. The only difference in our situations is that I have known I was adopted since I was a child.

January gaped at him with wide eyes.

"You look shocked."

She nodded in agreement, not uttering a word. Finally, she asked in a hushed voice, "Is that why you inherited the ranch and became the executor of the estate?"

He shrugged. "That's the only thing that makes sense. I don't understand what happened before we were adopted, that's brought us here, but I hope we can figure this out."

Not only did January want to solve this mystery, she also wanted to know why he was so determined for her to sell the house. Their lives were intertwined: Each inherited part of this vast estate, each was adopted. "I'm stunned." She sat down on the bed and stared at him. "So we are in this together, huh?"

Ben nodded. "I'm sorry I don't have any answers for you."

"I feel like Calico is trying to tell us something. Do you think her locket has anything to do with this? She seemed to be touching it."

"January, I don't want to believe in ghosts, let alone try to interpret what a figment of our imaginations conjured up!"

"She is real! If we put our psychic abilities together, I'm sure she'll come back to us. Do you realize that the only time she's appeared is when you're near? Maybe she's trying to tell you something."

"No way!" Ben exclaimed, walking toward the door.

January looked around the room. "I am going to make cleaning this room my priority. If all goes well, I'll move in here over the weekend."

"I wish you wouldn't do that. What if the ghost comes back?"

She laughed. "Don't you understand? That's what I want! And this is from the man who doesn't believe in ghosts...what a hoot!"

"Well, let's just say I've seen some very remarkable things happening around this house today."

"I'd be more concerned if Calico doesn't come back. I feel strongly she has the answers we need," January said under her breath and walked into the hallway. Cathy was hurrying down the hallway toward the stairway that connected with the kitchen. "Cathy," January called to the housekeeper. "How long have you been upstairs?"

"I was putting the clean bedding in our room upstairs. I suppose ten minutes or so."

Ben stepped around January and asked, "Did you see or hear anything strange?"

"Like what?"

"Well, how about a ghost?" January whispered.

Cathy broke into a smile. "You two really had me going for a minute. A ghost? Get real!" When January and Ben remained serious, she stopped laughing. "You are kidding me aren't you?"

January shook her head.

"Ghosts! What will you bring up next?" Cathy waved her hand as if she was dismissing the thought then headed back toward the back stairway.

"Do you see what I mean?" January asked and brushed her bangs out of her eyes in annoyance. "She blows me off without taking me seriously. Damn, that annoys me!"

"I wonder what she's up to?"

"It's hard to tell, but I'm going to watch her," she spoke with conviction.

CHAPTER 5

January sat on the rich floral cushions covering the window seat that looked out over the front of the house and leaned back to enjoy the fruits of her efforts. She had put the finishing touches to the master bedroom right on schedule.

Jim had worked for two days on the bay window that accommodated the window seat. He had stripped the broken window of plywood, replaced the panes and overhauled the brass handle. Now she could open the window and let in the fresh spring air, fresh with the fragrance of pine. The aroma was heady as it flooded into the room.

January wanted to feel the sunshine on her body. She walked to the door leading to the balcony overlooking the sunken rose garden below. The view was glorious. She could see the bend of the river. The water level was low, but it trickled over the small rocks worn smooth by decades of water motion. Tall Cottonwood trees stood majestically at the bank and groves of Cedar covered the hills and grew from the edge of the river. At the crest of a hill stood a white stone gleaming in the light. So bright that it hurt her eyes as she stared at it. January was held spellbound by the glistening light that reflected from the water and struck the stone. It reminded her of a grave marker.

Who would bury someone out there? Maybe she'd ask Ben. He'd called her at the motel last night offering to help her after he closed the office for the day. The thought of being near him caused her stomach to tighten with anticipation. If only he'd quit badgering her to sell the mansion. He was persistent; she could give him that much.

Even though the sun was warm, there was still a chill to the spring air. January hugged her arms to her body and took one last look around before stepping back into her bedroom.

The room was beautiful—even more than she could have imagined and it gave her the feeling of looking back at a better time of life. Carved wooden frames surrounded floral oil paintings and gave the room a feminine air.

She had found a hand-knotted canopy netting tucked in the back of the linen closet in the hallway and she had just finished stretching the diamond patterned material over the dome of the antique cherry wood bed.

Touching the fresh, ivory-colored paint, she delighted in the hue that enhanced the built-in shelves in the corners of the room. She had gone through the kitchen selecting numerous items: a decorative teapot, a cup, and saucer, flower vases, anything to fill the bare shelves. She removed the elegant silver picture frame from the shelf and lovingly stroked the deep etching. Polishing it had taken a few hours, but it was worth all her efforts.

The room was ready for her. All she had to do was check out of the motel and drag her suitcases up here. All of the hard work getting this room fixed-up was geared toward her moving from the motel, but she admitted to herself that she was a little bit apprehensive. She had to contact Calico, and now, everything was in place for her to do just that, a raw panic filled her soul.

Dismal feelings of fear and anxiety weren't part of January's character and she wasn't about to let them in now. She was in control of her destiny; after all, she had come this far, hadn't she?

She walked from the room and skipped down the back stairway and into the kitchen. Cathy was standing in front of the stove stirring the contents of a large pot. "I'm going to the motel to get my luggage," she told the Cathy, but the woman continued her kitchen chores without response. "It shouldn't take very long. I'll be back for lunch." January moved toward the stove and looked in the pan. She breathed in the smell of chili powder, tomatoes, and onion. "Chili! It looks and smells wonderful."

"I'm glad you like it," Cathy muttered in a sluggish, monotone.

What a sad person Cathy was. January wanted to be a friend to the woman, but each time she tried to draw Cathy into a conversation, she seemed to shrink away. At least January hadn't overheard any more angry outbursts from her. That made for an uncomfortable situation.

January walked out the French door leading to the flagstone patio at the back of the house. Spring flowers and an assortment of daffodils, tulips, crocuses were beginning to bloom in the overgrown garden. She had been working so hard on the house that she hadn't had time to clear the flower garden. She could ask Jim, but he had been too busy with work of necessity. Oh well, the house was shaping up, and now with Ben's help, it should go much more quickly. Just thinking of Ben caused January's stomach to flip with excitement. She loved being around him. Turning the key in the ignition, she started the car.

BEN HAD CANCELED HIS afternoon appointments and drove three miles out to his cabin on the shoreline of Lake Garrison, to change into work clothes. Helping January work on her project was...was what? Fun! And now, he was driving toward the river—toward January.

As the road curved, he saw the front of the house. January was tugging her suitcase out of the trunk of her car. She was good to her word; apparently, she had finished the bedroom and was moving into the house just as she had predicted. Damn! She was getting much too attached to the mansion, and her plan was quickly becoming a reality.

Willis representatives were starting to drag their feet regarding the sale of his ranch. They had planned to use the vast ranch as the national headquarters for Willis Beef. The cattle they raised were noted for its lean meat because the cattle grazed the land and were not fattened in feedlots. Garrison had shipping available for the cattle, but without the mansion, they had nowhere for their executives to stay. Throwing his car into park, he jerked open the door and hurried to January's side, pulling the large suitcase from her hand. "Hey! Let me help you."

She turned in the direction of his voice, her eyes wide with surprise. "Thanks, I'll get the smaller bag from the trunk."

Ben climbed the steps, dropping the luggage on the freshly painted porch and opened the heavy wooden door. Leaded glass in a fan-shape replaced the wood he had nailed over the naked hole.

January stepped inside and nearly bumped into Cathy who stopped in her tracks. Surprise registered on Cathy's face, and she said, "What are you doing here, Ben? I thought you were coming later."

"I was...and...I am. I have a free afternoon so..." Why was Cathy questioning him like this? And why did she look so—nervous?

She shifted her weight from one foot to the other. Her hands were behind her back, and she kept glancing up the stairs. He knew January didn't trust her and now he was beginning to feel the same way. Had he made a mistake in finding this couple to work here?

"Cathy! You look fantastic. Are you going out?" January quizzed and set the small travel case on the dark brown quarry tile foyer floor. Cathy had changed from her tattered jeans, and now she wore dark blue slacks and an expensive looking pale blue sweater, the cut looked expensive. Instead of her usual ponytail, she wore her naturally straight hair down around her shoulder, and she had curled it.

Cathy nodded her head and answered, "Yes, if that's OK with you. I have an appointment. Your lunch is ready and simmering on the stove. There's plenty if Ben wants to stay."

"Thanks. Have a good time." January spoke sincerely. "You deserve an afternoon off. I'm going to spend the afternoon unpacking and getting settled into my room. Is Jim going with you?"

"No. He had to go down to Cheyenne. Remember? He called while you were out and said the washers were in, but the dryers won't be there until tomorrow afternoon. I thought I would make use this time for myself. I'll see you in the morning."

Apprehension filled her. Tonight would be her first to stay in the house. The word alone crept along the edges of her mind, and a shudder zipped up her spine. She turned to Ben and said, "Let's get these cases upstairs. I'm anxious to show you the room and what I've done to it."

A slight movement caused January to look through the foyer and into the dining room. The garden through the French doors caught her eye, and he stared after her. "My God!" She cried and hurried across the room, Ben and Cathy close behind. "Who did this?"

The garden had been cleared of debris and the dark soil cultivated.

I've been here all morning, and I saw no one outside. Maybe, Jim, had some of his friends work on it." Cathy was clearly puzzled. She paced to the window and back to the middle of the room. "I don't know who could have done this. Not Jim...he was down in the basement getting ready for the new laundry before he left for Cheyenne." Cathy looked around the room as if searching for answers in the walls and ceiling. "This place gets creepier by the day."

"What's that supposed to mean?" January asked. She recognized Cathy's feelings, but admitting she was standing in the middle of a haunted house was another story.

"You know what the problem is and so do I," Cathy said, hysteria threatening to spill over into her voice. "Everyone in Garrison thinks you are crazy for opening the house. They think you should leave well enough alone. They are worried that you will stir up things, again."

"Again?" January's turned toward Cathy, her eyes wide with wonder. "What are you talking about?"

Cathy clenched and unclenched her hands at her sides demonstrating her fear. "At the market... they asked me if I'd seen ghosts?"

"They?" Ben interjected. His jaw throbbed with impatience.

"Y'know, people in general. Everyone knows I live and work here... and they ask."

"What do you tell them?"

"Uh...ah..." She avoided Ben's eyes.

"Cathy. Answer me." His voice tone was demanding but somehow comforting at the same time.

"I-I've told them t-that this place is haunted. And I've even seen the ghost. She glides around near the corners of the rooms. The other day she tried to push me down the stairs. If my hands had been full, well...I would have been killed."

"Oh, no," January mumbled under her breath. "How are we ever going to convince anyone to stay here if they think it's haunted?"

"You could sell it." Ben blurted.

January shook her head. "Who would want to buy a haunted house? If a ghost cleared the garden," she said raising her hands and head toward the ceiling. "Thank you!" Turning from the window, she walked back to the foyer.

"See you tomorrow," Cathy said, escaping quickly to the hallway to get her jacket.

Ben sighed and followed January up the stairs. He could see down into the foyer and a little way into the drawing room on one side and into the dining room on the other as he ascended the stairs. Near the doorway leading to the dining room a wispy fog formed as he watched. Here we go again, he thought.

But this time he wasn't fearful. Every time he came to the house it seemed the ghost appeared, haunting him. He didn't want to admit it to January, but he was starting to believe in ghosts—Calico, at least. It appeared that she was following Cathy out of the room.

Was January right? Was the ghost appearing only when he was around? And if so, why?

"Because you are trying to sell the mansion, you fool!"

The force of the words reverberated throughout his mind, heart and into the marrow of his bones. His knees felt like rubber, and he grabbed on to the banister so not to careen to the floor. Calico was speaking directly to him! How could she know about the sale? He shook his head to clear his thoughts and hurried up the stairs and caught up with January as she reached for the door of the master bedroom.

"Hey, slow-poke. I didn't think that bag was so heavy it would slow you down that much on the stairs. Are you out of shape?" she asked, January's sweet voice filled with lilting laughter. She opened the master bedroom door, standing back to let Ben enter. "So...what do you think?" Her voice trailed off when she saw his ashen face. "What's the matter with you? You're white as a ghost."

"Good choice of words, Jan!"

She snapped around to look at him. "Did you see her?"

"N-no." He lied, not ready to admit to this to her. "This place makes me nervous, especially when you're not around."

January peered at him. He hated it when she narrowed her eyes and stared. He felt like she was trying to get a psychic feeling or...God forbid, read his mind!

"This room is beautiful!" he said, trying to change the subject. And it really was beautiful, that much wasn't a lie. The once drab, lackluster room was a riot of color. The light from the bay window danced around the room, glistening over the tchotchkes on the shelves. He shook his head and turned to January. "You've really outdone yourself."

She smiled. "Thanks. I hoped you'd like it. This room makes me happy. Oh...come and look at the bathroom!"

Ben smiled to himself. January was so animated and filled with life. Gone was her reserved demeanor. He was utterly captivated by her now that he had seen the real person inside under her protective shell. He felt like she had cast a spell over him. He was afraid to analyze his feelings, they were changing so fast. He hated to bring up the sale of the house, again, but he had to do this. If he didn't produce her signature on the papers soon, he would lose the ranch sale!

"January was on her knees looking behind the cushions on the window seat. "Damn! I can't find my earrings," she asked breathlessly.

"When did you lose them?"

"Just now. I took them off and laid them on the table by your chair before I went to the motel for my things."

"Then why are you looking under the cushions?"

January took a deep, steadying breath and closed her eyes. "Since they weren't there, I thought I'd check everywhere."

"January, sit back down, I need to talk to you," he said in a low tone that gave his voice a demanding air. "I know you don't want me to keep bringing this up, badgering you about the subject, but I have an offer on the house."

She turned around and glared at him. "No way! I don't want to sell it." Dropping down on the cheerful padding she adjusted the pillow behind her back. Her movements were choppy with anger. "How can you keep asking me this? I refuse to sell the house, do you hear me? I will not sell...not now...not ever! You don't understand how much this house means to me." She was nearly yelling with frustration.

"January..."

"You're wasting your breath."

Ben pulled a wing chair in front of the window and sat down. She had drawn her legs up under her, and the unbecoming skirt covered her feet. He wondered at her strange choice of clothing. She was tiny, but the heavy material swamped her causing her to look chubby. If she was trying to make herself appear unattractive, it wasn't working. He felt the first stirrings of desire.

He returned his thoughts to the matter at hand. How was he going to keep January from finding out just how far the proposed sale had progressed? It was nearly complete and had been since before she arrived in Garrison; January needed to sign the papers, that was it.

"OK, so talk," he said leaning back in the chair and stretching his long legs in front of him. "Tell me why you want to do this."

She looked out the window and took a shaky breath. "We come from such different backgrounds, you and I. I've had to work at a nursing home as an assistant to the nurse. I've emptied bedpans, made beds and given baths to the elderly residents. I didn't have the money to attend a four year school and get a degree as a Registered Nurse, but I've studied at libraries on my hours off in a different field."

Ben nodded as she spoke. He knew of her background and the way she lived. Frugality was a necessity. He had admired her even before they had met. She probably learned more living her life than he had in his four years of college. She didn't have a great deal of money. That was why he thought she would jump at a chance to sell the property. Maybe that was his real problem...he hadn't thought!

January was very bright and quite capable of running the retreat. He wanted her to succeed at this enterprise. To hell with his father. She most probably could control the money left in the estate upkeep account. And a lot of it remained. The maintenance on the old house only used the interest on the money. January would have it all, and she would get to keep it even if she sold the house.

"Are you sure you want to do this?" he asked.

"I've developed all the plans. I might open an elegant restaurant right here in conjunction with the retreat. My kitchen is more than adequate. The only food offered around this town is hamburgers or steaks. I could do much better than that!"

"But why in this particular house?"

"The idea is hard to explain, but I can see the dining room in operation." Her eyes became glassy as she watched the picture unfold. "I'm standing at an antique desk talking to a patron who is going on about how enjoyable the dining room atmosphere was. I know I can make it successful if you give me a chance. I'm tired of working graveyard shifts and lifting people in and out of bed. I want my own business, and now I have a good start. What's wrong with that?"

"First of all, if you want this...this author's retreat your writers wouldn't want all the noise and people that a restaurant brings with it."

"Ahhh...but it would bring in money to augment the retreat." Her eyes were dancing with delight, and Ben's heart started beating quickly. He was becoming angrier by the minute. Why had he thought January was different? She wanted money just the same as Audra. She was trying to raise the price of the house with all the cleaning and restoration. He felt confused and hurt. Was this a game all women played? Heaven knew he hadn't had much experience with women. Money, money, money!

"A fancy restaurant! Out in the middle of nowhere? No way!"

"Why not? Tell me."

"The community is very unpretentious as a whole. You wouldn't have enough customers to support it."

She leaned forward in the window seat passionately. "I disagree. First of all, the only reason there isn't a full-scale restaurant in Garrison is that no one has been courageous enough to start one. Second, if there was such a place with an area for meetings and for drinks, I'm sure it could be a success. Look at the smaller communities around. Surely, there are some business people in all the areas that would use my restaurant facilities."

"And the retreat?"

"This house is so large...privacy wouldn't be an issue!"

"I won't give you the money for this project," Ben uttered angrily.

January jumped up and jammed her fists to her hips and railed at him, "Ha! You won't give me the money? You have no choice. As a matter-of-fact, I know to the penny, exactly how much money was in the maintenance account."

"Was in the account? What do you mean, January?" The blood vessels in his neck stood out, and he felt his face flush with anger. She had more nerve than he had ever imagined.

"Since the money is mine and just sitting in the old account, I moved the money so that I can tell use it. I don't need your approval. This is my house, my money, and my project. Now, I don't mind you hanging around here..." she smiled at him softly as if she knew some buried secret then continued, "but I'm taking control and I want to know why you want me to sell this house so badly?"

Ben felt his stomach fall like jumping off the high cliffs that edged Lake Garrison. He couldn't tell her that he needed his father's approval of a job well done. She wouldn't understand because he couldn't understand these feelings himself. And fear was the other motivation. He was afraid of what she would find if she searched this house.

There had to be some reason why they each of them had inherited the old estate. Was the ghost trying to show them, tell them something? He didn't want to find out. Leave well enough alone was his motto. That's what this situation needed. Yes—sell the place and leave well enough alone.

The silence in the room was formidable. He could hear the train clanging as it crossed the trestle that spanned the river to the north of town and the soft lapping sound of the river as it splashed over the boulders blocking its path downstream.

January's bright eyes clouded over and tears threatened to spill over onto her dark, thick lashes. She turned her head as if to look out the window but surreptitiously wiped the tears before they tumbled off her lashes and onto her smooth cheeks.

"I think you should go now," she said in a shaky voice that suggested both disappointment and hurt.

"I'm sorry. I didn't mean to hurt you..." he offered. Why was he apologizing? He hadn't done anything! "I'll call you and we can..."

"...Just go. Please!"

Ben stood and walked out the bedroom door, down the stairway and out the front door. Damn it all; it would be a cold day in hell before he would step foot back into this house. January had made him feel peculiar. It was a strange mixture of lust and yearning as well as love and adoration. He had hurt her beyond description, and as much as he regretted that, he wanted to push her away. He was more afraid of his ripening feelings for her than the possibilities of the house being haunted.

CHAPTER 6

After Ben left, January continued to sit and stare at the door as if willing him to return. She knew he wouldn't come back; he was much too angry. How had that argument started? She wondered. It was so stupid it seemed unreal. Now that he had shown how cunning and deceitful he could be, she understood why he had been so eager to help her. He wanted to stay around and tempt her to sell the house. It had nothing personal to do with her after all.

Her heart wouldn't accept that he only wanted the house. It made her sad to think that this budding relationship was ending before it had a chance to begin. One thing was apparent, he caused her body to surge with feeling in a way she'd never before allowed.

January raised her fingers to her lips and directed her thoughts there. The memory of Ben's kisses brought back the tingling, burning sensations to the tender skin. Was the kiss only a ploy to get her to sell the house? She didn't think so...it had felt genuine. How could someone fake something so intimate? If he was inquisitive about a relationship with her, why had he left without discussing the missing earrings? No. He must think her plain and unbecoming. The disagreement gave him the opportunity to escape.

As preposterous as it was, how could she have gone from awe-struck to despondent in such a short amount of time? The way her emotions soared, then plummeted, she felt as if she had been on a roller coaster ride. The sob escaping her throat sounded forlorn and melancholy in the thick-walled room. It matched the sad, desolate emptiness of her heart and seemed to linger in the air like warm breath on a frigid morning.

She was so confused, not only by this strange inheritance but by Ben Cottier himself. First, he seemed angry she was in Garrison and that she wanted to keep the house. Next, he was open and friendly, acting as if he wanted a relationship with her now, he argued with her, hurting her to her soul. So...that was it! Then it dawned on her that he was afraid of her...afraid! It took putting all of his emotions together to show her what was happening. Simply put, he liked her too much. Hadn't he said, after all, that Audra had hurt and humiliated him? Yes! Ben felt the intensity of the chemical reaction that had developed between them.

Her chest felt tense and her muscles throbbed from her unnatural position in the window seat. Rising, she ambled to the bathroom and switched on the light. Her tear-streaked reflection bounded back at her from the large mirror. She looked terrible. Her eyes were red and puffy and her hair hung in strings in front of her eyes.

The extra large bathtub looked so inviting. She had dreamed of this moment when cleaning the bathroom. Oh, to soak and forget this mess she found herself in. She brushed her hair from her forehead and wiped the tears from her eyes. Yes. A bath was just what she needed.

Her suitcase was still where Ben had dropped it, and she tugged it over to the bed. After a struggle, she laid it on the bed, unzipped it and hunted for her toiletries. She used little makeup because she had clear skin and her thick, black lashes needed no assistance from mascara. Her only weakness was the creamy rose-colored blusher and matching lipstick that gave her pale skin required brightness.

After searching for the jug of bubble bath, an inexpensive brand sold door-to-door by housewives looking to make some extra money, she returned to the bathroom. She twisted the bath faucets on full to allow a rushing stream of water and dumped a triple amount of bubble bath into the tub under the force of the water. In a short time, thick foam filled the tub. She turned off the water and started to pull her sweater over her head when she heard footsteps near the door.

Certain it must be Ben returning to her, her heart surged in her chest. "Ben..." She spoke expectantly, then turned. It was Calico.

The entity was framed in the bathroom doorway. The ghost appeared proud and upright, her chin finely chiseled and graceful and her neck finely proportioned. January could see her so clearly. The blue, calico-print dress had puffed sleeves reaching to her waist, and around her neck, she wore the gold necklace. January's knees trembled from the shock, and she dropped down on the edge of the tub.

Fear was the farthest thing from her mind. A feeling of peace surrounded her.

"Oh, Calico," she said sorrowfully, "I wish you could tell me why you're here. I'm so confused."

The longer she watched, the more substantial Calico's face became. January had always presumed ghosts were translucent, but not this one. There was something about Calico...her eyes...they were...January shook her head. Familiar is the only word that came to mind.

You have grown into such a beautiful woman. I've missed you so.

The words echoed in her mind. Were they her own? Where had they come from...Calico? Absolutely. They edged into her mind telepathically, but their imprint upon her emotions felt real and sharp as a hot iron. A sob stuck in January's throat. Surely, this person had to be someone that had known her. January had the uneasy feeling that Calico was inspecting her. She looked at the ghost as she hovered about a foot off the floor. Abruptly, a sparkling object slowly floated around Calico, flew through the air and dropped at January's feet. But still, January was not afraid.

Take care.

There is danger here. Beware of the other one.

January opened her hand. She held a beautiful Cameo necklace, the one Calico had worn.

The room began to spin, and January felt herself slip into the darkness. Deeper and deeper until she felt the heavy air sweep her into its depth, like miles of salty sea.

Sometime later, January began to rouse in a gray fog. Where was she? Lights around the mirror made the reflections from the shiny walls to look distorted; she began to shiver uncontrollably and found she was reclining in the bathtub. The water felt lukewarm, and the few remaining bubbles that hadn't dissolved were clinging to the edge of the marble.

She didn't remember getting undressed and climbing into the bath, but she must have done so for her clothes were folded neatly on the counter as she always had done before bathing.

She sat up with a start. Calico had been here. She remembered seeing her clearly, but more than that, the ghost's face was an older version of her own.

That did it! She shook her head to rid the cobwebs that lingered from her strange sleep. She had to find background information on the Call family. She knew the information she needed was somewhere. The first place she would search was the house. Then she would check out the newspaper office. This had been a wealthy family. There must be articles about them somewhere, and photographs, if she was fortunate to find a clue to the whereabouts. She dried her skin vigorously, bringing the blood to the surface that caused it to turn pink and once dry, wrapped the thick towel around her body.

Entering the bedroom reminded her of the argument she'd had with Ben, and her stomach did a flip-flop. She wanted to tell him about this experience, but no—that was impossible, he was pushing her away, and she didn't want to frighten him more. This was something she had to keep to herself.

January walked to the closet. She was glad her mother had gone through her apartment and sent her a box of clothing. Now, she was pleased to have different garments to wear. The long skirts she usually wore hindered her as she cleaned and restored the house, and besides, she looked right down peculiar in this town. It didn't matter anyway; she didn't plan to attract any men.

January smiled. Her mom had been thoroughly stunned when she told her that she was staying in Wyoming. Shocked, but happy for her just the same. She had wanted January to change her life and proceed with her writing. Mom was the biggest fan of her developing psychic abilities.

Tugging on the flaps until they opened, January dug through the contents of the box and pulled out a pair of faded jeans and an embroidered denim shirt, clothing from her past. It had been over six years since she had worn these. She laughed aloud. Denim would never go out of style.

Living in Denver, she had to guard her body. Here...well, she could be herself. This deep honesty was something she hadn't done for a long, long time. Maybe she could find out who she really was.

She dropped the towel and looked at her naked body in the mirror. Her breasts were still perky and full, and her tiny waist accentuated her narrow hips, making them appear curvier than they actually were.

Digging around in the suitcase, she retrieved her lingerie, lacy red panties and matching bra. Even though she had dressed in a plain manner, underneath, she'd been all woman.

The jeans and shirt fit perfectly. The pants hugged her slim thighs and flowed over the curve of her rounded hips and derrière while the shirt fit loosely, but her full breasts were the prominent feature.

She had to get out of these clothes! How could she go downtown looking this way? People would whisper about her. Stop it, she warned herself. Most women would love to be so curvaceous. Just because she'd had a few bad relationships didn't mean every man would treat her disrespectfully, like a prostitute. January thought she could hide herself, but now she understood that she was only hiding from herself.

After much deliberation, January unpacked all of her old clothing. They were pretty well worn, but it was fun to dig in the closet and come up with different items to wear.

January spent all of her time working on the house. It took her nearly two weeks before she found the time to go to the newspaper office. Waking early, realized she needed to get out of the house. She had missed some beautiful days, and she wanted nothing better than to drink in the fresh air.

She jumped out of bed, bathed and got ready for her exploration. She wore a fringed jacket with her jeans and tennis shoes. She felt 'dressed-up' for her trip downtown to the Garrison Gazette to inquire about old articles about the Call family and anything she could find about Pine Gables itself.

The weather was beautiful so she took off on foot. On each street, she saw people working in their yards, and they waved to her and said hello. What had caused her narrow-minded views of small-town life? It indeed hadn't been a fair assessment. This little town wrapped itself around her heart.

It only took her a few minutes to walk to the heart of downtown Garrison. The home of the Garrison Gazette was small and narrow. As January opened the door and took a few steps inside the business the phone was ringing. She stood at the counter listening to the continuous ring. No one appeared to help her or to answer the nerve-wracking phone! There was a computer sitting on a desk and racks of large binders against the far wall. A paste-up table sat beside the desk.

She stood there, not knowing if she should stay or go. Just when she was about to leave, a man entered the office from a back room at the same time the telephone stopped ringing. He wore his hair long, pulled back in a ponytail. A handlebar mustache was the focal point of his features and his thick glasses were smudged and dusty. He looked annoyed.

Tossing his jacket in the chair behind the desk, he looked at her over the top of his glasses. "What can I do for you? You want a subscription to the paper?"

"No. I need to find some information on an old family of this area and I thought this would be..."

"...Not today," he said sharply, interrupting her. "Our issue goes to press tonight. I don't have time for this."

January was taken back by his unexpected behavior. "When is a good time for you?" she asked.

"I'm here in the office every Thursday and Friday. Not tomorrow, though." He turned, flipped a switch and a light glowed from under the glass of a paste-up table. He directed his attention to aligning an advertisement at the bottom of the paper.

He continued to work and as she watched him an idea formed.

"Excuse me, again," January said, leaning over the counter.

The man didn't speak but looked up at her impatiently.

"I see your advertisement section. I need to place an ad. Can you get it in this edition?"

His eyebrows rose in interest. "Umm, that depends." He stared at her.

"So? What does it depend on?" January was getting impatient. Must she pull each response from him? This man was rude and irritating. She guessed she had a lot to learn about rural life, but rude was rude!

"Make it short. I don't have much space left." He tossed a clipboard toward her and returned to his paste-up.

She scribbled on the poor quality copy and handed the ad back to him. "Maybe we should start over," she spoke softly, and in the friendliest tone she could muster. If she was going to be living here, she needed all the friends she could get. She extended her hand. "I'm January Mohr. I recently moved..."

"...So you're the one, huh?" He kept his eyes on her ad. "I can't believe you're putting in an ad to hire workers at that spook house. Who are you gonna get to stay there? No one will want to, if they have good sense, that is."

January opened her purse to get her wallet. She looked up at the man, her gaze throwing him daggers. Her temper flared easily, and she had to fight it back. This man infuriated her. Was everyone against her opening the retreat at Pine Gables? First Ben, now, this stranger. "Mr., Mr..." She was at a loss for what to call him. He didn't wear a nametag, and there was no indication of his title on the desk.

"Danvers, Ma'am. Lionel. Lionel Danvers. I'm the editor, publisher, and go-fer of this paper." He looked into her eyes and a grin played at the corners of his mouth.

"Well, Mr. Danvers, why do you think opening a retreat in this town is so humorous?" she asked, trying to calm her temper and act friendly. Maybe he could tell her something about the house. She didn't need to alienate him.

"It's just its history. The place has been sitting there empty for who knows how long. It has a reputation."

"Hum. I see, but it's a beautiful home, and I've hired people to make repairs on both the inside and outside of the mansion. I'm sure most of its reputation problems stem from rumors."

Mr. Danvers looked at her ad and twisted one long strand of the mustache as he contemplated her advertisement. "I have a thought. I'm always looking for news articles. Why don't I publish this ad and do an article on your new business opening in town?"

"That sounds great!" January cried, hoping this would be the start of the community accepting her into its fold. "Since your newspaper is nearly ready to go to press, should I assume the interview will be sometime next week?"

The editor nodded and flipped through his desk calendar. "I'll come over from Wyland on Tuesday. How about two o'clock?"

What had changed his mind about her house? "Fine...fine," she muttered, only half hearing his end of the conversation because she was so deep in thought. "I thought you only worked on Thursday and Friday."

"I'm only in this office those two days. I split my time between the other small papers.

"I still have my questions about finding background information on the Call family. Do you have any old articles here?"

"No, not here. There may be something at the main office in Wyland. That's where we keep all the back issues. The paper has over one hundred years of back issues."

"Really," she said and felt her heart sink. How was she going to have time to investigate this? It could take months of sorting through papers to find one article! "Don't you have the papers on microfilm?"

Danvers shook his head and offered, "No. I've talked about doing that, but I can't afford it. The Wyland office is headquarters of three papers, all of which are small."

"That's a lot of papers. Have all three been in operation for this extended length of time?"

"No. The Garrison Gazette is the only one."

January breathed a sigh of relief. Possibly, she could find something, anything to get her start at finding the reason she inherited the estate.

"The Henley Herald and the Platte Telegram have been around longer, 120 years."

Her heart continued its fall toward her feet. She envisioned herself setting in a room with papers stacked from floor to the ceiling.

"Tell you what I can do. If I run across something, I'll bring it along with me next week. Possibly work it into the article."

"Thank you, Mr. Danvers," she said and paid her bill. "I'll look forward to seeing you next week."

THE SUN HAD SET WHEN she approached the house. January had spent the day wandering around the town. She found herself walking down a narrow highway that had information signs announcing the "Oregon Trail Ruts." She followed the road for about a mile and walked up a hill to a parking lot. As she followed the trail, she imagined she was one of the women walking beside her husband's covered wagon. Deep grooves from the multitude of wagons that traversed this old trail were worn into the limestone hill.

She scoured the area and found other places where the wagon wheels had cut into the ground. On she went, exploring until she thought her legs were nearly too shaky to hold her. She needed to rest for a while. She used her last bit of strength to climb a boulder so she could sit on the flat top. The sun was warm and relaxing. January leaned back, her hands supporting her weight and her legs dangling over the limestone rock. She closed her eyes and soaked up the sun.

Since she arrived in Garrison, her life had changed so much. She no longer had to work at the nursing home. Her days were, now, filled with buckets of paint. Smiling to herself, she opened her eyes before she ended up falling asleep and careening off her perch. The sight her eyes took in shocked her. She was looking at her house from the other side of the river. The property was absolutely beautiful Jim's hard work had really paid off—the once overgrown drive was cleared of weeds and the bushes were trimmed back. Now, it was simple to navigate and wouldn't scratch the sides of a car.

She looked at the house; really looked at it, as if she were a customer. Would she be frightened off by the possibility of staying in a haunted house? She didn't think she would be, but she was different from a lot of people.

Ben would be apprehensive to spend the night...no, he would be scared stiff. January really missed him, but not his incessant badgering her to sell the house.

She had to give this idea a good try. Her goal was one year. Hopefully, it would be a moderate success by that time. And the restaurant would bring many customers even if the retreat failed.

January studied the rocks in the river. If she was careful, she could walk right across and be home. Carefully, she stuck her foot out and nudged the first rock. It stayed tight in the gravely base of the shallow river. If she slipped off, the only thing that could happen was the water might cover her foot. She stepped from rock to rock, and in a matter of moments, she stood in her circular driveway.

She skipped up the steps still appraising the house. It was beautiful. The cream-colored stones stopped under the windows on the first floor, and narrow lap siding continued to the attic. Jim had painted it light yellow and the trim dusty blue. The pale colors did much to dispel the melancholy feeling surrounding the house. And the bushes in front of the foundation were trimmed back, no longer overgrown and blocking the windows of the first floor.

Unlocking the door, she went in, flipping the switch near the door. Light flooded the entryway from the antique lead crystal chandelier above her. What an experience cleaning that object had been. Jim had to devise scaffolding to raise him high enough to take down the chandelier, and he and Cathy had cleaned for two days before all the beaded strands sparkled.

She was getting used to the silence of the house, even enjoying the peacefulness. With only two more rooms to complete, she was feeling quite contented and pleased with herself.

The ad in the local newspaper caused her to think about the whole aspect of advertising her Writer's Inn. That was how she was beginning to think of it. The word mansion was too austere and retreat also...vague. Yes. Pine Gables Writer's Inn was perfect.

A rumbling in her stomach returned her attention to the present. There was little she could do about getting customers to the inn right at this moment. She took her billfold and car keys out of her purse and walked through the kitchen and out the back door. There was no way she could walk to the grocery store. Besides, she needed junk food!

When she returned from the store, she unloaded her plastic bags, filled the coffee maker with water and measured out the fragrant, ground coffee into a filter. Cathy had left her a casserole in the refrigerator and January turned the dial on the electric oven and slid the dish to the center of the rack.

At the only grocery store in town, she found two magazines featuring bed and breakfast inns. She sat down at the small round table. Leafing through the magazines, she was amazed at the beautiful homes in the issues. She looked around the kitchen. This house was just as gorgeous, she thought. What was it they did to bring the rooms to life? Studying the glossy pages again, she noticed each picture had flowers somewhere.

January took a stoneware mug from a peg under the cabinet and slid the cup under the stream of coffee and carefully filled it from the pot. She looked out to the garden. Would there be enough flowers to cut during the summer? Probably not, she thought, and if there were, she wouldn't have time to build arrangements. She walked out into the garden and sat on a cement bench, taking in the beauty. This area would be her favorite place on the ground floor, one she would use every chance she got.

She poured over the magazines for the rest of the evening making notes on a legal pad. Ideas flew from her mind to the paper. She listed: Printer—business cards, florist—prices, Inns—place an ad, and—enter contest.

The contest required a photograph of the outside of the house and numerous interior shots and a two hundred fifty word essay about the historical or particular interest of the inn. She could handle that! The first prize would be a Godsend. It provided free advertising in the magazine, and the inn would be registered nationally with the notation it was the winner of a nationwide contest as the *finest* retreat.

She looked at her watch. It was late, and her eyes felt rough and scratchy. Turning off the lights on the main floor, she walked up the back stairway, down the long hall, and into her room.

After getting ready for bed, she took out a mystery from the stand beside the bed and stretched, enjoying the feel of the smooth sheets. Many nights, recently, she had fallen asleep while reading. She thumbed through the pages and found the last paragraph she remembered reading and entered into the novel.

January snapped awake with a jerk. She must have fallen asleep. Her heart was hammering in her chest from awakening so quickly. The feeble glow of early dawn filtered through the window. In a sweat of fear, feeling almost paralyzed, she reached for the lamp switch. She heard an audible click as she operated the lamp, but nothing happened. The room remained in the gloom of early morning.

She became aware of steps outside her door in the hallway. Tossing the covers off, she slipped out of bed and slid into her slippers. Grabbing her robe from the foot of the bed, she headed for the door.

Bang!

Her hand froze on the brass doorknob. It sounded as if a piece of furniture had lifted and fallen over her head in the ballroom. She became rigid with fear. Calico hadn't frightened her, but this was different, remarkably different. She was alone in the house. Accumulating all her courage, she twisted the knob and threw open the door to find no one there. She wasn't surprised at that, either.

"Whew," she said aloud in an attempt to rid herself of the tension that had been building since she had awakened. What was she going to do? Were the sounds her imagination?

The thought had no more than passed her consciousness when Calico appeared in front of her. The ghost looked anxious and motioned to her to follow. Around the specter was the unmistakable sweet smell of violets, coupled with a feeling of intense cold and a kind of humming vibration. Each time she perceived the ghost, the experience was different.

January followed for only a few steps then, she stopped. The sound of footsteps that had awakened her returned along with the sound of a woman sobbing. Calico began to ascended non-existent stairs. Had there initially been stairs in this location, she wondered. Slowly, feeling her way down the hall, step by step, in the dark, she could hear the rustle of her robe. The sound of footsteps faded, but the sobs grew louder, more regular. January climbed the back stairway.

The stairway was narrow and dusty, and she had to repress the urge to sneeze, fearing frightening away anyone that was lurking in the ballroom. This didn't seem like a haunting, it felt more like she was trapped in one of her psychic dreams. Twisting the skin on the back of her hand until pain shot through the area convinced her she wasn't dreaming.

The open ballroom was dark, and January hadn't ventured into that area of the house when she was cleaning. Cathy said she wanted to do this. Something had held her back, not fear, but apprehension. Now, she wished she knew her way around. It was difficult to see in the large room. It wasn't dark, exactly—more diffused pink and gold of the rising sun.

Calico hovered in the far corner of the room. This time, she looked as pale and translucent as she had the first time January saw her in the basement.

Furniture, trunks, and boxes filled the room, and she had to twist and turn, sometimes changing her course to another area of the room. As she neared the corner, Calico held up her hands as if to ward January away, but she continued her progress across the remaining distance of the room.

A woman lay face down on the floor, the side of her face exposed for view. Her skin was ashen. She was beautiful. Her long black hair mingled with the black sweater and slacks making it difficult to determine just how long the hair really was.

January knelt down and touched her.

"Are you all right?" January asked, but gained no response. Calico had faded away, frightening January making her legs grow weak. How had the woman entered the house, and besides that, why was she here? January couldn't tell if she was dead or alive. *Call 911 or call Ben?*

January ran back down the stairs and entered her bedroom in record time. Reaching for the cell phone she had left in the room, she poised her shaking finger above the number pad. Ben, she'd call him. Would he come? She had to try.

Opening her contacts, she located Ben's office number.

Damn!

She touched the number and hoped the phone was synced up with his cell phone.

She counted as the phone rung eight times. As she took the receiver from her ear to hang up, she heard a mumbling voice say, "Hello."

"Ben! Is that you?"

"Umm...yeah. Who is this?" He sounded barely awake, his voice thick with sleep.

"It's January. I'm sorry to call you like this, but there is a...woman in my attic. I think she may be...dead. Please! Can you come? I really need your help!"

"January? My God, what happened? Oh, never mind I'll be right there. It takes fifteen minutes for me to get into town. Call 911, and I'll be right there." She heard the click of the phone disconnecting.

She hurriedly punched in 911 and got the calm voice of the dispatcher in Wyland. After she recounted the incident, January rushed downstairs. She wanted to be there when the police arrived.

Seven minutes had never felt so long. She paced back and forth in the entry. She heard the ambulance and saw the flashing lights long before she opened the door to let in the paramedics.

An older man, his thick white hair mussed from sleep asked, "Where is the patient?"

She started up the stairway as Ben burst through the front door. "Jan...where is she?"

"Up here. Follow us."

Moments later, a light flashed on in the ballroom when Ben flipped the switch. January hurried to the far corner.

"Oh, my God!" she cried. The corner was empty. Suddenly, January knew deep inside this had been a vision, but an image of what?

CHAPTER 7

Ben stared into the empty corner. "January. There's nothing here!" He looked down at her. Her eyes grew wide, pleading and glittering with tears as she looked at him.

"I did see her. I really did. She was lying right here." Her voice sounded high-pitched, nearly out of control to herself. She bent her head and closed her eyes. The faint light reflected off her spiky, white-blonde hair and it glowed in the dark corner as she shook her head in confusion.

He stood behind her and grasped her upper arms. He could feel her trembling. "I don't understand what took place, but the police will want to know what happened. The only thing in the corner was a box full of Christmas ornaments. It lay on its side. Glass spheres, broken from the fall, littered the floor.

He turned away from her, feeling confused. He had to ask her the question that was building; threatening to tear out of his mind and wreak emotional havoc on both him and January. "I-I have to ask you this. Don't fly off the handle now, but why did you call me? There's nobody here. No sign there ever was a body. Was this a scheme just to get me over here?"

She shook her head dejectedly, "No! I would never do that." She grabbed his arm and swung him around to face her. "I don't care if you believe me or not. I know what I saw. Whether it was real or, a vision is beside the point. I called you because I needed your help."

He hated to hurt her again, but he had to have the answers. This woman confused him to the core of his being.

The emergency crew burst into the attic. "Where's the patient?" Concern etched lines into the face of a middle age EMT as he scanned the attic, then his gaze flew to January as he took in her shape under the thin robe.

"Whoa! Hold up there, Gale." Ben raised his hand, palm facing out toward the man. "There's been a mistake. There's no patient. I think Miss Mohr became upset when she was awakened from a deep sleep. See the box over here? I think it fell off the table. You can see where mice have been chewing on it." Ben looked at the woman by his side and watched her heave a sigh of relief. He guided Gale to the dark corner. "When she came up here," he continued, "she was frightened—didn't know where the lights were and began looking around in the dark. I think the body she thought she saw was nothing more than shadows."

"'Spose you must be right—no one's over there, for sure." The EMT looked over his shoulder as two uniformed officers entered the attic.

Leaving Gale, Ben walked to the doorway leading to the attic to relate his version of January's tale to Sheriff Kincaid, but the official wasn't as easily swayed as the EMT's and insisted on searching the attic.

Finally, convinced there hadn't been a homicide, he sternly spoke to January, "Young lady, around these parts we don't call for help just because we're scared.

"But I..."

"Stop," he interrupted, "I suggest you get a handle on your imagination or go back to the motel. If you can't stay in this house without overreacting—move." He whirled on his heel and marched toward the door.

Without making eye contact, the Sheriff motioned to his deputy to follow. The deputy looked at January and gave her a reassuring nod before following his supervisor. Sympathy showed in his kindly eyes.

"Let's get out of here. It's too gloomy," Ben said as he guided her to the doorway. "Come on. It's over."

She looked over her shoulder to the dark, dismal corner and started shaking uncontrollably. "I'm glad you think it's over, but I know differently."

"What's wrong?" Ben questioned. He relaxed now that the others were out of the attic. "Are you all right?"

"Sure, I'm alright. I find dead people all the time!"

He saw tears balanced against the ridge of her lower lashes and they threatened to spill over the edge and down her smooth cheeks, but she turned and wiped away the tears before they splashed.

Reaching out he turned her toward him and pulled her against his chest. Slowly consoling her, he rubbed his hand over her back, trying to comfort her, relax her. "I know, I know. There is something strange going on here. I'm going to stay here with you for the next few nights."

"Y-you can't d-do that. I'll be fine."

"No, you won't be fine at all. Something is going on, and I'm going to stay." He kept his arm around her as they edged slowly down the stairs. When they reached the kitchen, he pulled a chair out with the toe of his worn cowboy boot and eased January onto the chair. Looking around the room, he spotted the coffee maker.

"Where do you keep your coffee and filters?" He asked.

January directed him to the cabinet by the stove, and he measured out the coffee into the brown, Earth-friendly filters, and slid the container back into its spot. After pushing the switch to the *on,* he dropped bread into the four-hole toaster and walked over to the table where January was sitting, her head in her hands.

January's look of despondency pulled at his heart. Not only was the problem of her visions draining to her, but also, but his attitude about the house also couldn't be doing her any good. He dragged out a chair for himself with his foot, the legs made a soft squeaking sound as they scraped on the tile floor. Ben eased himself into it.

"The house is looking great," he said, not wanting to aggravate her by talking about whatever it was that happened earlier.

"Thanks," she spoke flatly.

Ben looked at her. She kept her head down, not showing him her eyes so he couldn't determine her feelings. Was she angry? Hurt? Or what?

Maybe his earlier observation was totally wrong. "Do you want to talk about it?"

She didn't answer but nodded her head slightly in an affirmative motion. She was wearing a long dusty-pink robe and matching slippers. The material was thin and shiny and followed the curves of her body.

Ben stood when the toast popped from between the red-hot elements. He reached out and stroked her hair. "Like I told you before, I've decided to stay here with you. You-you shouldn't be alone."

She looked up into his eyes and could see his sincerity. "Why do you want to stay here?" January asked, confused by his change of heart. Why was he so willing to stay with her; protect her from the unknown happenings at the mansion? She wouldn't complain, but she wondered about his attitude change.

He poured them each a mug of coffee and placed the hot, buttery toast in the middle of the table. "Jan, I've faced the fact that something unnatural is happening here. I can't explain the garden cleaning itself or your flight from the ladder. I believe there is a spirit at work here and I-I want to be here with you, to protect you."

"OK. But I don't want to hear one word from you about selling this mansion. Can we agree on this?"

Ben nodded and smiled at her. "Tell me what happened."

January stared into her coffee cup, then took a long sip. The moments passed without a word spoken. He had just decided she wasn't up to talking about it when she raised her eyes to his.

"It was strange, so strange that I'm afraid you won't believe me," she spoke and walked across the kitchen and retrieved the coffee carafe, returned to the table and poured Ben another cup and topped-off hers. She rinsed the pot out while recanting the episode to him.

"Yeah right. When it comes to you, darling, nothing is sane, especially me." Ben said, then laughed lightly. "It sounds as if Calico was warning you against going into that corner. Can you explain that?"

January shook her head and frowned.

"Y'know that really surprises me," Ben said, a grin breaking across his face. "And you're supposed to be a psychic."

"It makes me wonder, too!" She cried and walked to the window near the table, hugging her arms around herself in a protective manner and looked outside. "Ever since I've come to Garrison, my psychic skills are shot." Deep in thought, she stared into the fresh spring morning.

"Maybe you're trying too hard."

"Umm, that's a possibility. Without it, I feel lost." She returned her attention to Ben. She wanted to forget the ghost and the haunting taking place in her house.

"I'll be glad when the weather warms enough to sit on the patio for morning coffee." She turned and leaned against the wall. More to herself than to Ben she continued, "I've always felt my psychic abilities were a nuisance and I wanted it to fade and leave me alone. Now, I feel so confused. The guidance I've lived with for so many years has changed. I feel that it hasn't deserted me, only become confused."

Ben nodded, he didn't want to say anything to her and break the spell. He didn't claim to know much about visions, as a matter-of-fact, he had once jokingly called psychics "psychotics," but he wondered if all the bizarre happenings around here weren't a direct cause of her extrasensory aptitude. Ben took a long sip of coffee, giving her time to formulate her thoughts. He could hardly believe she felt her abilities had decreased since she'd arrived. He wondered how strong she had been in Denver.

"I pinched myself earlier when I was going up the stairs to the attic. It was as if I was in a dream, in a vision, but I could feel the pain." She dropped into the chair as a wave of stress-induced fatigue overpowered her. She reached for a slice of toast and studied the pattern of butter in the center.

"You think it was a psychic vision?"

Taking a bite from the toast, she chewed slowly, nodding her head. "Yeah, I suppose that is exactly what happened. Nothing else makes any sense."

"I agree with you. Otherwise, the body would have been there. Can you describe the woman?"

January shook her head as to clear the cobwebs from her mind. Standing, she took her plate to the sink and began rinsing the dish. "Well, the woman was beautiful. She wore black wool slacks and a black Angora sweater. Her hair..."

"...Slacks?" Ben quizzed, his dark eyes bulged behind his wire-frame glasses. "I thought you were going to tell me she wore a long dress in an 1800's style, an old-timey dress. This woman sounds modern."

"She was quite fashionable, actually. And her long, black hair was everywhere and made her face seem milk-white in contrast."

Ben nodded as January spoke. This was what she needed to do, talk.

January stared through the kitchen door and into the dining room. Her eyes looked heavy and sightless. Could she see the sunlight streaming into the room or the dust sparkles dancing in the glow? "The ghost was there. She guided me to the ballroom."

Ben nodded but didn't look at her. He felt her examining him. "Now you won't stay here, will you?"

January laughed.

"What's so funny?" Ben asked.

"Nothing! I-I think we are letting this get out of hand. Now, everyone in town will believe I'm crazy. Do you think I'm crazy, too?"

Ben stretched his long legs and slumped in the chair. He folded his hands over his tight stomach and looked at her for a long time. "Do you really need to ask that? Of course, I don't think you're unbalanced. I thought I was cracked when I was in the house, but not now. Jan we really have to find out what this is all about."

She nodded in agreement. "Yeah, I know. Have you got any ideas about how we can do that?"

"No."

"I-I have started something," she stammered, "I placed an ad for staff in the local newspaper, and they are doing an article on the house next week. I think that might bring some skeletons out of the closet."

"It might do just that. You're right; it sounds like a good enough place to start." Ben pinched the dimple in his chin as he contemplated his next words. "I just wonder if we're prepared for what the article could start."

January stood and walked to the sink. She dampened a cloth and returned to the table to wipe up the last traces of crumbs from the wooden surface. "Mr. Danvers is going to look for old articles about the house, too. I just hope he'll find something."

Ben walked across the kitchen and up to the sink, standing beside January as she rinsed the crumbs down the drain. "Why don't you get dressed? I think we need to get out of here a while. What do you want the Clark's working on today?"

"Oh, they know, but they're out of town for a few days. Now that Jim has finished the outside of the house and the laundry room in the basement, he can concentrate on the last two bedrooms. Can you believe we're almost done? This house wasn't nearly as bad to fix as I feared."

"Do you need to buy bedding and towels? That kind stuff?"

January shook her head. "I ordered it from a vendor I met when I was staying at the motel. I got institutional quality bath towels and matching terry robes for the rooms. The linen is high quality, but more expensive. I thought it would last a lot longer that way."

She looked up at him, afraid he would be angry with her. After all, he had wanted her to sell the mansion, and she wasn't really sure of his sincerity. How was he going to handle the fact that the house was only a couple weeks from completion? Her goal was at hand.

Now, all she had to do was find paying customers. If everyone thought the house haunted, she was afraid that would drive her business away.

"Sounds like you're ready. I hope the article brings you business."

"I'm entering a contest in a bed and breakfast magazine, as well." She told him about the requirements. "If I win, the free advertising could really help."

"Could I see that magazine?"

"Sure, it's on the desk in the foyer. Go ahead and look at it while I dress. Let me know if you find something you feel we can incorporate here at the house. I need all the ideas I can get!" With that, she turned and walked from the room.

When she came back downstairs dressed in black jeans and a white blouse edged in black satin embroidery, Ben had her laptop computer booted up and was hunched over the thing typing furiously.

"What are you doing?" January asked. She hadn't known she was possessive about her computer, but watching Ben navigate the program she had difficulty with, was unsettling.

He looked up at her over the top of his glasses. "Pull up a chair. I have a plan."

She picked up a wooden chair and carried it to the desk. After getting all the floors in the house sanded and refinished, she wasn't about to drag a chair and chance scratching the shiny surface.

In a few minutes, Ben looked up and used his dazzling smile on her. "I'm done. That magazine solved all my problems."

"Do you mind sharing your good news?"

"Well, I don't know exactly how to begin."

January smiled back at him. "Just begin, and we'll put it together once it's all out on the table."

"You were right all along. I was pressing you to sell the mansion. I felt my ranch sale would fall through if you kept the mansion." Ben kept his eyes on the computer screen.

January squeezed his arm and turned his upper body toward her. "Look at me."

Ben snapped his gaze toward her.

"Explain, please."

He sighed, ran his fingers through his hair, brushing back the graying sides behind his ears. "Willis Beef is the company buying the ranch. Their headquarters, right now, is in Miami. Many of their executives will have to spend time in Garrison once they begin with their project to relocate most of the company here, and to make matters worse, most of the administrative staff doesn't want to move here. They will commute."

"So?"

This would take all day at the rate he was going. "So, they wanted to buy the mansion to give their people a place to stay while they conducted business here."

"Oh! That makes sense. But Ben, I'm not interested in selling, remember?"

"I know. Now I've stumbled on the perfect situation, thanks to your magazines here. The Willis people don't need to buy the mansion. They can stay here, at your Inn. It's such a simple solution I should have thought of it immediately."

Excitement pulsed through her and she threw her arms around Ben's neck and planted a kiss on his lips. "This is perfect. I was worried if I'd have customers in this small community. But would all of these people bode well for the retreat? It would be more of a Bed and Breakfast!"

"You're right. Damn! I thought that was the solution."

January stood and paced the room. "Wait. How many people would be here at one time?"

"No more than three, but every couple of weeks or so, they would change."

"Okay, how about this idea, we have the carriage house sitting out there at the back of the garden. What if we cleaned it up, stocked the kitchen and let the company use it? That way, the business people would be out of the writer's hair."

"January! You're a genius. That's the perfect solution. Yes! This will work for both of us!" Ben jumped up, grabbed January in his arms and whirled her around. Their gazes locked and as Ben set January's feet back on the floor, their lips met as if drawn by a deep hunger that neither of them expected.

January pushed against his shoulders and broke the kiss. "Stop, please. You make thinking impossible."

"You want to think at a time like this?"

"Yes," she said and sat back down. "Come on, I want to talk to you about something else...oh, no!"

"What's the matter?" Ben graciously sat.

"Jim and Cathy are living out there. They've spent so much time cleaning, repairing, and whatnot, they might quit if I ask them to move in here."

Ben slowly shook his head. "That's just a chance we'll have to take. Is there enough money in the account to give them a nice raise? I know, I'll give them a bonus for all the work they've done to the carriage house!"

"That may work. I think Cathy is motivated by money. Now, about that question, I was about to ask. Is there anyone in town that could install a computer network?"

"A computer network? Why?"

"Well, my customers are writers. If they had access to a computer in their room, this would enhance their work."

"Are you sure? A network's clunky. All they need is wireless service. Everyone has their own laptops and even now you can write documents with voice on your cell phone. If we got a powerful service, it would work in the guest house as well."

"Thanks for all your ideas. Working all this time, and many of my hours on the graveyard shifts, I've lost track of technology."

"It does move quickly," Ben said, then looked under the desk and saw that the printer was attached to the computer, pressed a couple of keys on the keyboard and began printing his notes. "Don't thank me yet, we'll have to present this idea to them, make them want to go for this." January's eyebrows knitted with concern. "You *do* think they'll go for it, don't you?"

"It's their only option if they want their cattle to graze on the finest grass Wyoming has to offer. After all, the mansion isn't for sale."

"Thank you." She mouthed the words because her throat was so tight from the emotion that she couldn't squeeze them out and her eyes filled with tears.

Ben kissed the tip of her nose. "Quit blubbering and get a jacket."

"Where are we going?"

"To my office. I have to call Willis Beef and set our plan in motion. Then I need to go out to my place and pack a bag. I absolutely refuse to allow you to stay alone in this house."

"But I'm not alone, most of the time."

Ben shrugged. "It's the times when they aren't here that I worry about." He stroked her cheek with the tip of his index finger. "I won't stay if you really don't want me to."

She gave him a half smile. "I have lots of room here, and it can be a little frightening even when Jim and Cathy are here. They can move in, and we'll make a suite for them on the third floor."

"Great! Shall we go?"

January stood and looked at the schoolhouse clock. "I'm not sure when Jim and Cathy will be back today, let me leave them a note. I'm expecting my linen order, and..."

"...Leave a note on the door to have them delivered to my office. Danica is there this afternoon. She can sign for them." Ben opened the door for her, and they walked out onto the front porch. The May sunshine was warm, but the breeze still was slightly chilly.

January skipped down the steps and got in the SUV. "Do you think this is going to work, Ben?"

"Why shouldn't it?" he asked as he turned the key in the ignition. "We have to look at it positively. It will come across in my voice when I call them."

Ben's office, a long narrow building with a rustic wooden front, was on Main Street, right across from the Post Office.

January followed him through the door. The phone was ringing when they entered. Ben raced through the lobby and into a narrow hall that led to the back of the building. So much for Danica working this afternoon.

She took in the office. It was nice. The fluffy gray carpet appeared nearly new, and so did the tapestry-patterned furniture that nestled in a corner and was arranged for easy conversation. The polished coffee table held an assortment of magazines. Situated in the other corner was the receptionist desk.

"Jan, come on back. I have Adam Willis on the line."

She took a deep breath and started down the hallway, the direction Ben had gone. There was a room to her right, but the door was closed. She followed the hall. It led directly to his office. The homey looking room had a fireplace and worn leather furniture. Whereas the outer office had a formal feeling, this room was comfortable and reflected a more relaxed atmosphere. A rugged coat tree that looked like a tree branch stood by the door. Ben's cowboy hat and infamous duster hung were suspended from individual twigs.

Tintype photographs and loops of rope sat on shelves. The coffee table in front of the worn leather couch was a pair of cowboy boots holding a sheet of glass. January felt comfortable in this room, just as she was becoming more comfortable with Ben himself.

Ben pointed to a leather chair that faced his desk inviting her to sit. "Just a minute, Adam. I have Miss Mohr here with me. I'll put the phone on speaker." He punched a button and hung up the receiver. "Can you hear me?"

"Sure can, Ben. Ms. Mohr, I'm happy you are in the office today."

January grimaced and shrugged when she looked over at Ben. This call made her uncomfortable. "Good morning," she said.

"Ben's told me you're not interested in selling the Call mansion. Is that right?" Adam Willis did not sound pleased.

"Yes, Mr. Willis. I have no intention of selling the mansion."

There was no sound coming across the line for a moment, then he said, "Ben told me about your project. He said there would be an Inn as well as a restaurant. Is this right?"

"Yes, but the restaurant idea is far from complete."

CHAPTER 8

"Good. Because I wouldn't be interested in that. Now, you are opening the first Sunday in June?"

"Yes, that's the plan." January was becoming aggravated. She felt like she was at a job interview.

"I'll agree to use your facility because I don't want all my plans ruined. Some of us will be there that night. We'll stay about a week. I'll send you a menu of what we decide to eat and..."

"Hold on there, Mr. Willis." January couldn't take any more of this, and she jumped to her feet. She paced back and forth in front of Ben's desk. She knew her voice sounded angry, but that was the way she felt. He was ordering her around! "I will be happy to take your reservation, but I insist we do this correctly! I will follow my business plan."

Ben looked at her, his eyes open wide with dismay. "What are you doing? He mouthed to her.

She held up a finger to her mouth to indicate she wanted him to be quiet. "I'll have the carriage house available, and I'm dropping the restaurant idea, but the food is up to your employees. The carriage house has a beautiful kitchen. Why don't you get with your staff and let me know how they would like the kitchen stocked, I'll include this service in my billing."

"Oh, it sounds like your plans are underway."

"Yes they are, sir, and I would be delighted to take your reservations, but I determine my services, not your company."

"Would it be possible to hire a chef on the off chance we would need to hold a dinner party there?"

"I'll have to think about it. We are limited in living in a small town as to whom we can hire. Can I get back to you on this?"

There was silence on the speakerphone and an occasional sound of papers moving when Adam Willis said, "All right. Give me your number, and I'll call in the reservation tomorrow. By the way, have you dispelled that foolish notion that your house being haunted?"

January and Ben looked at each other at a loss for words. "No," January said. "And I don't plan to. Many people want to stay there because it is haunted."

"Ah, um, I suppose a little flavor won't hurt us any. How much work does the carriage house need, anyway?"

"Very little. A married couple, my housekeeper and groundskeeper, have been living there. Call me after you speak to your employees." January gave him her phone number, then Ben put the receiver to his ear and disconnected the speaker to conclude his conversation.

Thirty minutes later, when he hung up, he stretched back in his chair and put his hands over his head. "I thought you'd blown it, but you took control of that man. I can hardly believe it. Adam Willis is accustomed to getting his way."

"Not when it comes to my house, he doesn't," she said firmly. "You should know that by now, Mr. Cottier." Her eyes sparkled and danced with delight.

The telephone rang. "Cottier Agency, Ben Cottier speaking. Oh, hello." He listened to the speaker on the other end of the line. What? We're on our way." Ben looked at January accusingly, then told her, "That was Cathy. Your order has arrived. In a semi."

The trip back to the house was a quiet one. January couldn't understand what was eating Ben. He had been happy when she had overcome Adam Willis' bossy attitude. Was he angry that she had ordered things for the house?

Ben pulled into January's driveway and stopped the vehicle. Before she got out, he asked, "How much stuff did you order?"

"I told you, already. I needed a lot, but not this much!" January opened the door and stepped out of the vehicle.

Ben followed her to the back of the truck. The delivery man was pushing a moving cart stacked high with boxes.

"Hello," January said, "This whole load surely isn't for me, is it?"

"Oh, no, ma'am. I'm afraid your housekeeper got the wrong idea. You have a lot though." He stepped around Ben and pushed his delivery up the sidewalk and starting unloading it on top of the other boxes that sat on the porch. There must have been thirty large boxes sitting by the door.

She couldn't read Ben's expression, but it seemed softer, almost embarrassed. "Come on. Let's get all of this into the house. I'm so excited! This is happening, isn't it?"

"Wow!"

"Wanna help?" January asked.

Ben shrugged. "I guess I'd better if you plan on entertaining guests in less than a month! And I'll offer my support when you talk to Jim and Cathy about moving from the carriage house."

"Moving? Moving where?" Cathy shrieked.

January and Ben stared at each other. Finally, January said, "Cathy, let's go in the house. Is Jim around?"

"Yes, he's in the kitchen." Her eyes were filled with tears.

January tenderly touched Cathy's arm, "It's okay, Cathy. Ben and I will join you in just a few minutes." She turned to the delivery man saying, "Just put the boxes inside the door. We'll take it from there." As she signed the tracking log, she watched Cathy enter the mansion. The woman looked forlorn and depressed.

A few minutes later, January and Ben entered the kitchen. As the door creaked open, Jim jumped up from his chair and began jabbering. "Here, come on in and have a sit, Cathy and I have coffee, you take cream don't you January?"

"Sure," January said as she slid into a vacant chair across the table from Cathy whom kept her gaze to the tabletop and didn't look up.

"I can get my own coffee." Ben walked to the counter and took a mug from the metal hook screwed into the underside of the cabinet.

When they all were settled around the table, January was the first to speak. "Okay, guys, I made a decision today, and it's going to affect both of you. I'm sorry I couldn't discuss this with you first. You deserve this consideration. I didn't have time to do anything but act on the decision. If this upsets you, I'm sorry."

Cathy looked up, her gaze searched January's. "You want us to leave, don't you? I knew this was too good to happen."

Her words caught January by surprise. "You like it here?" From the past episodes, January felt Cathy must have hated it at the mansion.

"Course we do!" Jim offered. "This is the best job we've ever had, and we were lookin' forward to those writer friends of yours coming here, taking over this old house. Yes, ma'am! We love it here."

"Will you still love it here if you move into the main house?" Ben asked, then took a sip of his coffee.

"What?" Cathy cried. "Move in here?"

January nodded. "We are going to use the carriage house for a business headquarters, but I want to give you two a raise, and a bonus for all the hard work you've put in on the carriage house."

Cathy glanced at her husband. "Jim, what do you think?"

"Sounds good to me, Cath, we could use the extra money." Then turning his gaze to January, he asked, "But where are we going to stay here?"

Ben looked at January. She nodded her approval for him to answer. "Okay, guys, it's like this. There is that large area on the third floor that's behind the ballroom. That would make a great apartment, don't you think? Maybe we could get a contractor in here, and they could get this fixed for you fast. We can time it with the opening of the carriage house. What do you think?"

Cathy ran her index finger over the rim of her mug. "That new place sounds good, if only you would guarantee that the ghost would leave us alone."

January felt her stomach flip. What could she say? Calico. "I don't know what I can do about this Cathy, but maybe you can get used to her? She's not evil, I know that. I think she wants us to recognize she's here with us."

Cathy took a deep breath and said, "I guess we have no other options, do we?"

"When do you suppose we need to get out of the carriage house?" Jim asked.

January shook her head. "I don't really know, but I'll keep you informed. Now about those raises and bonus..."

SUN STREAMING THROUGH the master bedroom window awakened January. She stretched happily and looked around her beautiful room. A year ago, she never would have envisioned this happening to her. Everything was falling into place, and she hoped that the meeting with Lionel Danvers tomorrow would set her on the right track for finding her benefactor.

A knock at her door sent her scurrying to adjust the covers over her then called, "come in!" The door swung open, and Ben entered the room.

"Good morning, sleepy one," he whispered.

"Hmmm...what time is it?" She asked Ben, turning to look at her little black alarm clock. "Nine-thirty?"

"That's what we get for staying up late last night. I had a good time seeing all that bedding piled-up in the drawing room. It looked like a huge slumber party!"

She threw the covers back and swung her legs over the side of the bed. Her feet didn't touch the floor from such a tall berth, and she had to use an oak step stool to climb in and out of bed.

"I'm glad you had a good time, but you have to leave the room so I can get dressed."

"What's the hurry?" he asked, taking a step toward the door leading to the balcony. "Wouldn't it be enjoyable to have breakfast out there this morning?"

"Yes, but for as much as I would love to do that, I can't." She watched his gaze drifted over her legs, and she shuddered. Reaching out for the step, she felt the texture of the wood against her feet as she stood. Grabbing her robe from the foot of the bed, she slipped it on and tied the sash. "Mrs. Beemer will be here in," she looked at the clock once again, "twenty minutes to help me hang the new window coverings. Now get out of here."

"OK, OK, you don't have to get testy." He walked nearer to her. "Did you sleep OK? No ghosts pulling you from your sweet dreams?"

"No. Not a ghost in sight." January giggled. She enjoyed seeing Ben first thing upon rising. His jeans rode low on his hips, and his open shirt showed his well-defined abdomen. A fine line of black hair trailed down behind the waistband. His body was confusing her poor virgin mind. On the one hand, she was afraid of him, and on the other, she was ripe with desire.

He stepped closer to her and grasped her thin arms and ran his hands down their length. He pulled her to him and pressed his mouth against hers. He smelled minty and tasted manly. Her robe and nightgown were thin, and she could feel the pounding of his heart and the extent of his desire as he pressed himself into her hip.

"Um," she groaned, her self-control was plummeting fast, and when he grasped her slim hips, and pulled her against him, she knew her virginity wasn't going to plague her much longer. Pulling from his embrace was the hardest thing she had ever done. Never had her body betrayed her this way. "Ben, please. I have to get dressed. Will you go watch for Mrs. Beemer?"

"Sure," he said, but he reached out and grasped the length of her hair and pulled her back for another kiss. His lips ground against hers, and she felt herself tremble with desire. Opening her lips to his, he slipped his tongue between them and slowly moved it across their fullness. He grasped both of her arms and pushed her away. "Damn, woman. You excite me like no other woman has. Get dressed and I'll see you downstairs." He closed the door softly behind him.

January's hand trembled when she grabbed a baggy denim jumper from the closet and a bulky red sweater from the chest. On went her protective outer layer, but she knew Ben had penetrated her heart and there was nothing she could do about that.

The doorbell pealed through the vast house setting off an echo in January's ears as she reached the landing between the first and second floors. She could see Ben open the door for the plump woman.

"Hello, Mrs. Beemer," January said as she ambled down the stairs. Ben looked at her quizzically noting her clothing. "I'm so excited to see the window coverings."

"Mr. Cottier?" The woman turned to him. "Would you go to the car and bring in the box of curtains from the back seat. It is a little difficult for me to lift, my old age you know."

January directed the woman to the drawing room, and she watched the woman take in the beautiful furnishings.

Ben took January's arm and whispered, "She's the biggest busy-body in town. We are going to be the hot topic."

January shrugged and walked toward Mrs. Beemer saying, "Would you like coffee and a sweet roll before we begin?"

"No, thanks."

She could see the way the chubby woman licked her lips that she was tempted. "Maybe when we take a break?

"I'm quite anxious to see my work hanging in front of these beautiful windows. You just don't know how many times I've driven out to this mansion and pined to see the inside of it again."

Ben brought the box into the room. "Where do you want to start?"

"How about this room first. I believe by the measurements you gave me, January, that these windows are larger than the panes in the dining room. If that's right, they are at the top."

"Yes, they are." January looked at the size tag the seamstress put on each panel.

Mrs. Beemer walked toward her box of handiwork.

Ben leaned against the doorjamb with his arms folded across his chest. "You ladies are going to have to wait a few minutes for me to get the ladder. You're not climbing on the furniture to reach the top of the windows. And besides, I'm not even letting you get on the ladder, Jan. Do you remember what happened the last time?"

Mrs. Beemer looked at her quizzically.

"I nearly fell off. If it hadn't been for..."

"...me," Ben interrupted. "She would have fallen. Why don't you show Mrs. Beemer around while I gather my things and I'll meet you in the drawing room."

"Never mind him, he gets real bossy!" January's words were light, but she threw daggers at him with her eyes.

"Well, dear, I find him charming. It's nice to have a man around to help out. Why don't you call me Alice? Mrs. Beemer sounds so old. I just joke about my age. Now, I really would like to see what you've done to the house."

January showed her the bedrooms and introduced her to Cathy who was making-up a room on the second floor. When Mrs. Beemer saw what January called the Blue Room, she squealed with delight. "This is the most beautiful room I've ever seen. I love the soft blue wall panels. This trim isn't white, is it?"

January shook her head. "Eggshell. I felt white was too stark."

Alice circled the room touching the tiny lace doily on the dresser and the lace lampshade. "Someday I'm going to make a weekend reservation, and this is the room I want to sleep in."

Touching the woman's shoulder, January drew her back to the hallway. "I'll be delighted to have you as a guest. There's something I want you to see. It's on the next floor. Would you like to take the elevator up?"

The woman nodded. The elevator was across the hallway and January reached out and punched the black button sitting in the middle of a steel plate. The door slid open silently. They stepped into the small enclosure, and the door closed softly around them. The machine was slow, and it took little time for them to reach the ballroom. "This is it," January said. She directed the woman to the horsehair cushions that lined the walls. "At some point, I would like to have new cushions made for these seats."

Alice shook her head. "I'm afraid my machine couldn't sew through this thick material." She stroked the old velvet.

"Oh, no, I don't want to save these. I want new cushions."

The older woman nodded her head. She understood. "We came to a dance here, once. I must have been, oh thirty-five at the time. That was when my dear Herman was still alive."

January looked at her with wide-eyed dismay. Here was someone who had been in the house before it was closed up.

"Who owned the house? Mr. Cottier and I have been searching for our benefactor, but all the records are sealed. You are the first person willing to talk to us about this."

"Oh! I didn't know it was a secret."

"I think the only people it's a secret from are Ben and me. Can you tell me the name of the owners when you were here?"

She nodded her head. "It was a miserable situation. Those poor people." She looked as if she remembered something distressful; her eyes filled with tears.

"Please, let's go downstairs and have a cup of coffee and maybe you can remember. Ben will want to hear all you have to say."

Ben was standing on the ladder in the drawing room when the women entered. "That was quick. I thought I'd be finished with this room before you got back down here."

"Ben, Alice knows the names of the people who lived here thirty years ago. Go get the coffee pot and cups. We have a lot to talk about." January tipped her head in the direction of the kitchen.

He scrambled off the ladder and raced from the room to do her bidding.

"I hope this won't be too upsetting for you."

"No. I just can't imagine why anyone thought the secret was safe."

Ben walked into the room with a tray of coffee necessities and a pile of individually wrapped sweet rolls. "Finally, we're going to hear something besides, "Sorry, I don't want to talk about this." He mimicked a feminine voice.

Alice visibly relaxed, and she took a roll from the tray and concentrated her efforts to tearing the bag.

January poured the woman coffee and handed it to her.

"The couple that lived here, the name was Ford. Alexander and, I can't recall." Alice took a bite of the roll, and downed it with the coffee. "It was something like Myra, no Mirna, oh, dear!"

January patted her hand. "That's all right. Go ahead and tell us what you remember. Maybe her name will come to you."

Mrs. Beemer smiled up and January. "There isn't much to tell you, really. The mister shot his misses, then himself in the library."

"Oh, my God!" January cried. She glanced at the library door then back to Alice. No wonder she couldn't make herself clean that room. If it weren't so beautiful, she'd consider closing it off.

Ben stood behind her and rubbed her shoulders as a show of support. "That's horrible. What happened then?"

The woman shook her head. "I don't know. The next thing anyone knew, the house was closed. Of course the man went to prison and I heard he died there. The Fords' had only lived here a few months, so we really didn't know too much about them. If I remember correctly, the grandmother owned the house at one time. Before the younger Ford's moved in. I'm sorry I can't remember more."

"Oh, no, Mrs. Beemer, that's great news for us. At least we have a name. It's another way to try and find out how we fit into this." Ben said. "Can you remember what year that was?

She sipped on the coffee and pondered his question. "The years have a tendency to blend together. Miranda! That was her name. It just popped into my head. January and Ben looked at each other and back to Alice.

"She seemed such a lonely girl. The mister was a lot older than she. I always thought that they had staged the dance so she could meet some people her age. It's too bad what happened to her." Finishing the coffee, she replaced the empty cup on the tray. "Sometimes I think that is why I've always come by this house. I felt so sorry for that sad, beautiful girl."

"I'm going to finish hanging those curtains." Ben walked toward the ladder. "Am I doing it right?" he said in a teasing voice.

The women laughed, and January stood to admire his work. "It looks fantastic. They look just as beautiful as I thought they would look, but it's from Mrs. Beemer's sewing, not your hanging expertise!"

It took a few hours to hang all the drapes. The seamstress had just left when the doorbell rang again. Thinking the woman had forgotten something, January threw open the door. "What did you forget?"

A silver-haired man gaped at her. "Miss Mohr?"

She nodded "Yes, may I help you."

"I'm Bennett Cottier, and I'm looking for my son."

"Oh, Mr. Cottier, come in!" She stepped aside to allow him to enter. He scoped the room without giving a clue as to what he thought.

"I take it Ben is here?" He clasped his hand behind his back and leaned toward her.

"Yes. I believe he's in the dining room. I'll get him." This man was trying to intimidate her; she wasn't going to let him do that to her. He might be Ben's father, but he was a stuffy, pompous man to her. She found Ben sitting on the floor looking at the curtain rod. "Jan, I'm glad you came in. I think they sent you defective hardware. Look at this, it's bent nearly in half!"

"Your father is here. I'm delivering his summons!"

"What? Dad, is here?"

"As big as life. You told me he was different, but, boy! He's in a class of his own."

"What does that mean?"

January spun around to face Bennett Cottier. "Uh," she uttered, at a loss for words.

"Dad, good to see you. I want you to meet January Mohr." Ben smiled at her and winked. "Jan, this is my father, Bennett Cottier Senior."

"We've met. I must say, this house is imposing. You have made quite a difference, Miss Mohr, quite a difference."

January picked up the screwdriver and twisted it in her hands. "Thanks. The inn is ready except for stocking the pantry and freezer. I'm going to rest for a couple of weeks. This redecorating has worn me out." She smiled sweetly at him, but he didn't change his stoic expression.

"I don't want to appear rude, Miss Mohr, but I came here to speak with my son. Would you excuse us, please."

She glanced at Ben and back to his father. The older man must be angry, she'd never seen anyone without personality. Well, maybe he did have character. Mean as a junkyard dog. When Calico was around, it wasn't as cold in the room as it was this very moment. "I'll be upstairs helping Cathy with the bedding." January turned on her heel and escaped from the room.

"Well, that girl is much prettier than I was led to believe. She really knows how to put a house together." Bennett said after January walked from the room. "What is this nonsense I hear about leasing rooms to the Willis people?"

"It's true. They have reservations here. It's the ideal solution." Ben gestured with his hands in a sweeping movement. "That way, January can keep her dreams, and Wills Beef will have a beautiful place for their executives to stay."

"Humph! That is wonderful for everyone except the Cottier Agency. Where do we fit into this? Do we get a percentage of the money for setting up this arrangement?"

Ben stood and faced his father. His heart beat against his ribs making it hard to take a breath. The blood rushed through his head. He had tried to make peace with his father, but it hadn't seemed to work. "No money, nothing! I wouldn't do that. You really don't understand my motives, do you? Do I have to use people to get ahead? No. The agency is making more money without that type of management!"

Bennett crossed his arms over his chest and paced back and forth in front of the fireplace. "Is that what you think I do? Use people?"

"Yes. You always have. Your style of business is it is *who* you know and what they can do for you,' mine is 'what can I do for you?' See the difference?"

"I think we have a problem. Is there any way to solve this, son?" Bennett looked sincere. His blue eyes softened. "I can't operate your way, and heaven knows you can't survive my way."

"I know, dad." Ben's tone softened. "I really don't try to get under your skin. I love you, but you need to find something to keep you busy besides poking your fingers into the business. I think that's the problem."

His father nodded in agreement. "It's just that I don't have anything to do. That idea you had about Audra would have been fine, except I asked her out and she turned me down flat. She said she was still in love with you. The woman's determined to get you back. I thought you should know."

Ben dropped into a chair. "She really said that?"

"Yes. Audra looks like she means business, too. I think you should know there are rumors out there about you and Miss Mohr. I think Audra has heard them, as well. That might be why she wants you back. Some women are like that."

Ben rested his face in his hands, then raked his fingers through his hair. "Damn! Have you got any idea how I'm to get rid of her?"

"You're asking me? No, son, this one is all up to you."

Bennett walked out of the room and met January coming down the broad stairway. "I'm glad to have finally met you, Miss Mohr." He opened the door and left.

"Ben, are you all right?" January hurried to him and kneeling beside him said, "What happened?" She saw his hands tighten in anger.

"Dad and I just don't share the same philosophies on how to run a business. I think he's softening a bit, but I won't stoop to his level just to make money. I won't do it!" He stared at the far wall looking thunderous, then he eased himself out of the chair. "Also, he told me that Audra said she wants me back. God! Doesn't she know she never had me?" His eyes searched hers.

"Some people don't take no for an answer, Ben."

"Yeah, I know, and Audra is one of those people. I'm glad I met you. Do you know how special you are to me, sweetheart?"

Her heart soared. Ben called her sweetheart!

"I have an idea. Can you get away for awhile? I want to go for a drive."

"But what about, oh, never mind, I'll tell Cathy. Do we have time for me to change my clothes before we go?" she questioned, looking down at her unbecoming attire. "I'm starting to like wearing jeans. I feel clumsy in this dress!"

"Yeah, but hurry. I need to get some air before I explode.

THE HILLS AROUND GARRISON Lake were covered with cedar trees. The fragrance coming through the open window of Ben's SUV nearly overwhelmed her. The road twisted through the hills for about three miles then, at the crest of a hill, January spotted the lake.

"Pull over," she said. "I want to take a picture of this."

Ben swerved to the side of the road and stomped on the brakes. Before the vehicle had stopped entirely, January threw open the door and jumped out. She pulled her cel lphone out and started to click. The view was spectacular. The water was calm and reflected the surrounding Cedar-covered hills off the glass-smooth lake. Birds chirped and called in the spring sunshine. She felt so alive and so invigorated as she climbed upon a large rock to change her viewpoint.

Never had she expected to enjoy the outdoors. So many sunny days had passed with her sleeping just so she could go to work night shift. The sun warmed her upturned face and heated her leather jacket.

January sat on top of a boulder hugging her knees to her chest and looked over the lake. All along the shoreline, cabins were tucked between the trees. They were hardly noticeable and blended into the landscape.

The sound of Ben's door shook her from the nature-induced coma. "I love this place, Ben! It's truly magnificent."

A bird chirped a mournful call into the crisp air. January turned to the sound. "What bird makes that sound?" She asked.

"That's a Meadowlark. A true sentinel to spring and my favorite bird as well. Look over there, on that fence wire."

She spotted a yellow-breasted bird with mottled gray wings. Raising the camera, she snapped just as the bird emitted its melodious trill. "I'll give you the picture when it's developed. You'll have a picture of springtime."

Leaning against the side of the vehicle he stared at January, then his face broke into a wide smile as he enjoyed her gaiety. It was a pleasant change from the oppression they shared when they were in the house with the ghost orchestrating their feelings. "I like you wearing jeans and boots. When did you start this?" He asked.

"Oh, my mother sent me a box of things I had packed away years ago. She thought I could use them when I'm painting and stuff. I went through the box and thought I'd fit in better in Garrison if I didn't look so darned different!"

"Y-you look so much more relaxed. You're beautiful."

She turned her head away from Ben's gaze in embarrassment. She wanted to look attractive and desirable, but it sure made her feel uncomfortable. He brought out feelings she had hidden for years. Not just unseen from others, but from herself, also. She wanted to look sexy and luscious, but she knew her flirting techniques had lain dormant for years if they had ever been there in the first place.

"Come on down from there. I want to show you something on down the road. If we have to stop every few minutes, we'll never get there."

"Well, you're the one that told me to bring my camera," she laughed and started her descent down the rock.

"Ohhh!" She shrieked. The drop from the top of the rock to the road below was farther than she had expected. She'd climbed onto the boulder from the side not realizing the height from the road. Seeing her peril, Ben rushed to her, grabbed her by the arms and broke her fall. January was light, but her fall threw him off-balance. He staggered backward, nearly toppling them both. Taking a step to the side, he regained his equilibrium. "Hey, we have to quit falling into each other like this. One of us is going to get hurt. Are you all right?" January looked up at him. His glasses sat crooked on his nose. He looked as if he had taken the brunt of her fall. They were standing chest to chest, and her breasts tingled from contact with his body. The feelings made breathing difficult. The woodsy aroma of his cologne and his sweet breath in her hair amplified the sensual sensitivity that coursed through her body.

She could feel his hands stroking her hair as he hugged her to him and the intense sensations made her knees shake. Suddenly, she wondered at her sanity and pulled herself from his embrace.

"I'm fine, but you're a sight." She reached up and straightened his glasses. She couldn't see his eyes for the sun reflected off the glass hiding his expression. Had he felt the connection between them when he held her, she wondered.

He lopped his arm over her shoulders and guided her back to the car. Y'know that big disagreement we had right after you moved here? I wanted to tell you that you weren't at fault, I was. I pushed you away because, because at that moment I felt too close to you. There is chemistry between us, young lady, and I-I'm afraid this is happening much too fast."

January turned and gazed at him, narrowing her eyes. A flush of red crept from the opening of his brightly colored Western shirt toward his face. He was serious! She'd never been around such a sensitive man, and she felt the stirrings of anger in her soul. That woman Audra should be ashamed of her actions. She had hurt Ben severely.

"Please, Ben, don't. I understand, really I do." January didn't want him to be uncomfortable around her. She could feel physical reaction between them and if it was half as strong for Ben, he had good reason to be fearful.

They sat in silence; the radio, tuned to a country music station, played softly in the background, barely audible above the crunch of the vehicle's tires on the gravel, as Ben drove along the narrow dirt road for a few minutes. At times, January held her breath as he navigated the steep inclines and switch back curves around the hills that edged the water.

"We're just about there," he said and turned the steering wheel sharply to his left crossing the center of the road. Evergreen trees and bushes surrounded the narrow dirt road they turned on to, and it angled down toward the water.

An A-frame house stood in the clearing near the edge of the water. The center of the A was completely filled with windows and cedar shakes covered the sides. From the road, she could see a wooden deck edging two sides of the building, and a wooden walkway led from the house to the edge of the water.

A sleek ski-boat was moored to the floating dock.

"This is my home," he spoke. Pride filled his voice. "I've lived here for nearly six years. I like the feeling of isolation and the great view of the lake and hills. Maybe I like it here because there is nothing to remind me of my father. This is my home."

When the vehicle stopped, January opened the door and ambled to the wooden walkway. "I find it hard to believe that you live here, or that anyone lives this way. I'm so accustomed to the city that I never really thought about alternate lifestyles."

"Surely, you know about people living in cabins in the mountains." Ben tipped his head back and laughed.

January spun on her heel and turned toward him. "I just meant this place is so unexpected. I hadn't thought about living near a lake, that's all!"

"I know what you meant," he said softly, then taking her by the arm he led her to the deck and the entry into the cabin. "I'm sorry for teasing you. You looked so sweet and sincere when you made that observation. I couldn't keep myself from laughing. I-I'm sorry. I keep saying that, don't I? But you are a breath of fresh air compared to..."

"Audra?"

Ben unlocked the door not facing January and whispered, "Yes."

"I understand why you're reluctant to talk about her, she's here with us most of the time anyway. I don't mind if you talk about her. That might be the best way to get her out of your system."

The door swung open, and January looked into the house. It seemed to be one large room. A stone fireplace dominated one wall of the living room and on the other side of the room was a small kitchen. The counter divided the room.

A wooden table sat in front of a glass wall that opened onto the deck. This side of the house overlooked the lake. "What's in that alcove at the end of your deck?" January asked, craning her head as she looked outside. She slipped off her jacket and laid it over the back of the chair.

"The hot tub. I haven't spent any time getting it ready for the season." He spoke absently as he looked through a stack of mail he had picked up at the Post Office.

The house was small, but it boasted a modern kitchen with microwave, double-door refrigerator with ice dispenser and a grill-type range. "I love this kitchen. You must like to cook."

"Well, I don't know about that. I like good food, so I grill vegetables and steaks. That's about the extent of my comprehension."

"Oh, I just thought..."

"The cabin came fully equipped. But you can use the appliances any time you want to."

"Gee, thanks! To tell you the truth, I'd rather use your hot tub, especially after a full day of painting ceilings."

Ben tossed the mail onto the middle of the table and said as he wiggled his eyebrows in a bawdy expression reminiscent of Groucho Marx, "I'd love to see you glistening wet in the water."

January's mouth flew open but not a sound rang out, and her face flushed red with embarrassment. At that moment she wondered what she had gotten herself into. Ben was in another league, no, he was entirely in the ozone compared to her limited experience.

"Uh, Ben, y-you..." January couldn't finish because her thought had evaporated from her head. Ben didn't know how his innuendo had affected her. She wanted to rush to his arms and kiss him, melt into him.

"Come here," he whispered as he removed his glasses, folded the bows and placed them in his breast pocket. "You are so irresistible."

January's mind screamed at her to remain where she was, but her feet moved of their own accord and brought her nearer to the man of her dreams. He looked sexy the way his hair toppled over his forehead, and his full lips glistened soft and inviting. Closer and closer to him she moved. She felt the pulling attraction as a magnet to metal.

A shuddering breath ripped through her as she entered his outstretched arms. He embraced her, holding her tight against this firm, lean body. His heart hammering in his chest jolted her frame, and his breath against her ear raised goose bumps down her arm and leg.

Turning his head, their lips met in a hesitant, delicate kiss as soft as butterfly wings. She raised her hands and gently guided her fingers through the back of his thick hair and pulled his head firmly against hers. The pressure encouraged him to continue. Slowly, he slid his tongue across her bottom lip then he gradually sucked it into his mouth parting her lips. She groaned with the pleasure.

Was this what she had been hiding from all of these years? she wondered. No. She was finally ready to accept a mature type of love. The vertiginous kiss left her feeling weak and as fragile as glass. She didn't want him to stop, and it took all of her strength and determination to pull away from his passion.

"Ben," she whispered, taking a step backward to distance herself from the swirling aura of lust that had surrounded them. "What's happening to us?"

Taking a deep breath, he blew the air from his chest causing the hair that lay across his damp forehead to move with force. "I have a really good idea...I," he stammered and caught himself before he declared his love for her. "...I want to make love to you."

CHAPTER 9

"What?" January whispered breathlessly.

"You heard me," Ben said and stepped closer to her. Their eyes met and locked. "I want to make love to you."

"Noooo. I-I'm..."

He took a step closer to her and January stepped back, thwarting his advance.

"I want to kiss you all over and trail my tongue across your naked back. I'll pleasure you until you scream with passion." His voice was deep, and the timbre shook the foundation of her determination.

No man had ever talked to her in this way. She felt her resolve weaken. She didn't want to give in. Not after all these years. Lord, but she wanted him. She had saved herself for the right man; hidden behind unattractive clothing hoping no one would notice. The only aspect she had neglected to think about was what she would do when 'Mr. Right' came along. She knew that Ben was the right man, but she was so afraid.

She looked at him through half-closed eyes. "Is this what "talk dirty to me" means?

His eyelids were heavy, filled with lust as he leveled his gaze at her. "Not even close, darling. You know it's inevitable."

January kept edging backward, and Ben continued his approach. Suddenly, she felt the end of the banister in the small of her back. The stairway, situated in the corner, trapped her.

Her only escape route was filled with the male animal that was stalking her. Her mind whirled with confusion. She'd never seen him overwhelmed with desire. Just being near him weakened her resolve. If she ran from Ben, would she regret her decision? She felt sure she would.

Silently, she begged and pleaded with her internal crystal ball to kick in, show her what to do. But of course, nothing happened.

"Come on." He caught his lower lip between his teeth, then let it slid back out. "Let me show you what love-making is all about.

An overwhelming wave of longing swept her into its current, and it carried her, step by step, to the loft on the upper floor that overlooked Garrison Lake.

As she entered the loft, she had reached the point of no return. The room reflected Ben's personality. A massive wooden frame surrounded the large bed that stood majestically on a platform. A romantic vision of them making love in the middle of his bed played in her mind like an erotic movie. The chimera made her breathless, and a deep shiver of anticipation oozed through her body making her gasp at the pleasure.

Ben followed her into the room and walked to the fireplace. He took a long match from the holder and snapped the match head with his thumbnail, and it sparked to life with a sulfuric flash. The firebox was filled with wood and readily leaped into flame when he touched the match to the wood chips under the logs.

Firelight reflected its glow in his dark eyes as he looked at her. "If you're ready for this, come here." His desire filled voice sounded coarse, but it was music to January's heart.

She acknowledged his challenge with a slight nod of her head and parted her lips, running her tongue softly over her full bottom lip. Ever so slowly she sauntered across the floor to a blues tune that floated in her mind.

Amusement shone Ben's eyes and a playful grin play at the corners of his mouth. "You're a surprise. One moment you're frightened, almost virginal, the next moment you turn into a wanton sex kitten. Which one are you?

January slid her arms up his broad chest and around his neck. As she entered his aura, she felt her body melt into his and become one. She tilted her head up to look into his eyes. The softness she saw there urged her on as she pressed her full breasts into his chest. He lowered his head toward hers and their lips molded together.

Brazenly, her hands slid down his back, over his tooled belt and across the pockets of his jeans. His firm rear tensed as she squeezed the solid flesh and pulled him toward her. She could feel his reaction to her advances against her stomach and at that moment, she lost her fear. The uncertainty of the situation didn't matter at all. It was replaced with desire; a desire so strong that it left her a quivering mass of flesh.

Pulling back from the kiss Ben looked deeply into her eyes. "You're a wanton woman." He dropped his hands from her arms and took a step back giving her the opportunity to change her mind. "Are you sure you're ready for this?"

January nodded. "I'm surer than I thought possible." Her shuddering breath gushed out. "Make love to me. Please."

LATER, THEY LAY TOGETHER, his arms surrounding her. January drifted to sleep on the thick cloud of contentment. She had never imagined the physical act of love could be, so life-changing. She felt like a different person. Everything about her had changed with her move.

Ben rolled onto his side and pulled her along with him. "Let's take a shower."

"Uh, well..." she stammered, self-conscious even though she'd been naked with the man for the last hour.

He pulled her into his chest and encircled her with his arms. Looking down at her he smiled softly, and his eyes looked into hers. His mind warned him not to keep his mouth shut, but he said, "You're beautiful. Don't be ashamed of your body." He sat up, looking down at her. "You were a virgin, weren't you?"

January nodded. "Yes. Does it matter?"

"Not really, but I would have taken more care with you if I'd have known."

"Do we have to talk about this now?" she asked, pulling the sheet up to her chin.

Ben smiled at her. "Come on. Let's go shower."

"I-I'm not accustomed to this. After all, you've seen my normal style clothing." She pulled the blanket from the foot of the bed and wrapped it around her.

He reached for her hand and tugged her along toward the door on the other side of the bed. "Even if you won't shower with me, at least I want you to see what I've done to the bathroom."

She followed him into the room. "Wow." She cried as she took in the dramatic sweep of hills. From her vantage point, she could see the far shore of the lake. "It's a lovely view."

"The panorama was the reason I bought the cabin from the elderly man that owned it. His wife died, and he had no interest in camping without her."

January raised her eyebrows in surprise. "Camping? I wouldn't think to stay in this beautiful house was even a distant cousin to camping."

"It was much more rustic when I bought it. The outhouse sat on the north edge of the property." He tipped back his head and laughed. "Let me show you the new privy."

He walked across the room and opened the door wider, and January walked into heaven. The bathtub sat in front of a wall of windows.

"Aren't you afraid of peeping-Tom?" She asked incredulously.

"No. You can see out, but no one can see in. Did you notice the ceiling here and in the bedroom?"

January shook her head, and a blush crept up from her chest to fan her cheeks. Once in his bedroom, she hadn't been aware of anything except Ben. She looked over her head as Ben pressed a button near an antique dresser that served as a sink cabinet. Near the center of the table, a recessed copper bowl gleamed in the brilliant light of the room. Engraved gold-colored faucets completed the distinctive sink.

Suddenly, the room became brighter as a shade rolled back from the ceiling. The roof of the lake-facing side of the cabin was glass.

January's mouth fell open in astonishment. "This—this is so dramatic." She only presumed she knew Ben and his tastes.

Ben shrugged and said, "Umm, I'd say it was unique. Actually, I built this during my rebellious period. I had just finished college and started working at the agency. I put all my free time and money into this house, against my father's wishes, I may add."

"Don't you get along with your father?" She asked. She noticed that Ben rarely talked about his family, but when he did, his reference was negative.

"Well, you met him. He seems to think he's the only one that can do anything right." Ben shook his head and pressed the button, and the covering slowly slid back over the glass.

"I'm sorry. Your parents gave you a rough time?"

"Just from my father. My mother died when I was small. Sometimes I wonder if things would be different if she had lived. Being adopted wasn't easy." His eyes took on a distant glow as memories from the past filled his mind. "Oh, well. There's little we can do to change things.

January nodded in agreement and drew the blanket tighter around her.

Ben edged closer to her and gently reached out, tipped her chin. He softly kissed her full lips. "I'll let you shower or use the tub, whichever you want, I'm going downstairs and start lunch. I'm starved! I'll shower when you finish."

She stood looking into the incredible room. "OK, I'll..." Ben had already left the bathroom.

Soaking in the tub sounded terrific, but there wasn't enough time to luxuriate in the steamy water. She wanted to hurry and help with lunch preparations.

January descended the stairs and watched Ben hover over the grill. The aroma of cooking steaks made her stomach lurch in response. After the long day unpacking boxes, the food would relax her as well as a long soak in the tub would have done.

"Oh, that smells good," January said walking into the kitchen.

"Are you hungry?"

"Yeah, I feel like I haven't eaten all day."

"You haven't!" he laughed and flipped the meat with a long-handled spatula and smoke rolled from the seared meat and into the vent in the middle of the appliance. "If you work on the salad the meal will be ready sooner. The vegetables are in the bottom drawer of the fridge."

After three trips back to the refrigerator, January had the sink full of vegetable bags.

"Do you realize, the only thing we have ever done, is eat?" she asked, her words coming in spurts as she beat the lettuce core against the middle of the sink that divided the tubs.

"No. We've done more than that," Ben chuckled taking an onion from the pile in the sink.

"Ben!" The meaning of what he said made her blush. Just what did a person do after sex? Do you talk about it? Ignore the reality that it happened?

"Was I that terrible?" She asked, then bent over to retrieve the pepper, not wanting to see his answer reflect in his eyes.

"At what? Oh," he uttered under his breath when he realized what she was alluding to. "No way!"

"But you recognized my inexperience."

"Sure, but that doesn't make you inferior. You were wonderful."

January tossed the salad with her fingers and carried the bowl to the table. She was uncomfortable with this conversation. "I just thought that, that..." Her voice was barely audible.

Ben brought the steak and baked potatoes on a platter and set it in the middle of the table. Southwestern design placemats held heavy black dinnerware and matching eating utensils. He dropped into the chair and looked at her searchingly.

"What did you think? Finish your thoughts."

How could she tell him that she wanted her partner to be in love before she committed her body to the relationship? She knew she loved Ben, but how did he really feel? Did he care for her? This was not the romance of her dreams. "This all took me by surprise. I didn't intend to...well, you know."

"God," he uttered with a moan and shook his head as he dropped the grilled meat onto the plate in front of her. "Quit analyzing this situation and just eat. You look starved."

"Ha! No one has ever hinted that I look starved. Fat, maybe. But not starved!" January laughed at that notion and heaped salad on her plate then took the Ranch dressing, turned it upside down and shook the bottle vigorously.

Ben stared at her, the piece of meat speared onto the tines of his fork stopped before it reached his mouth. "I can't believe that anyone would think that you're fat, for heaven's sake. You have the most luscious body. You're curvy and feminine. Not a clothes hanger woman. I like your figure much better than that type."

He finished taking the bite, chewed thoughtfully and chose his words carefully. "I don't want to be presumptions, but all you need is a change of clothing style. I like the stuff you're wearing today. Those long dresses and sweaters swamp you. You're too little for that."

"I'll think about it," January said. She valued Ben's opinions. After all, he dressed smartly even if he was living in a rural area. "Ben, if I decide to buy a new wardrobe, will you come along with me and give me your opinion?"

"Sure. That sounds like fun."

They ate in silence for the remainder of the meal then Ben said, "Have you explored this area yet?"

"Some, but not much."

"Good! We'll drive around until dark. I love giving the grand tour."

"I DIDN'T KNOW THAT the National Guard Training Site was so large," January said as they drove toward the guard on duty at the north gate.

Ben handed his driver's license to the uniformed man. "I've been around this so long I had forgotten what it must look like to someone else."

The guard waved them through and Ben easily accelerated the vehicle and drove toward the stone buildings that edged a grassy field. "This is the parade ground. During the summer, the Governor rides in an open Jeep though the platoons to inspect his troops."

"Can civilians come and watch all of this?"

Ben nodded and turned onto a dirt road that led up a steep hill. "Sure. I'll bring you."

When they popped over the top January gasped. A gigantic military airport commanded the hill. Army green transport planes and helicopters were everywhere.

January rolled down the window and allowed the fresh spring air into the interior of the SUV. She looked out over the town from their high perch. "It's beautiful down there. I can even see the roofline of the mansion." The trees were budding out more each day, it wouldn't be long and the roof of her house would be hidden by the growth.

A gentle breeze blew into the vehicle and filled the interior with its sweet fragrance.

Ben grinned. "This is the first time I've seen you so relaxed and unconcerned."

She brushed her hair out of her face. "That's the way I feel. You've made me so happy! Why are you looking at me that way?" January smiled shyly.

"I'm hesitant to tell you."

"I don't know why you should be."

"Jan, I'm afraid you'll revert back to being so painfully timid.

"Oh." She turned her head and looked out the window. The breeze caught her hair and fluffed through the soft strands. "You know me so well."

"I think you're the most beautiful person I've ever met. You have a good soul y'know?"

"Ben, this is embarrassing me. Quit talking about me and point out these sights you wanted me to see."

"OK, OK. But you have to learn to accept compliments because I'm going to give you lots of them." He leaned over and kissed her gently on the lips. "Ummm, you taste so good. Thanks for not pulling back."

"When did I ever pull back?" she laughed and lifted her arms to his shoulders and kissed him back. "Come on. Tell me about this town before the M.P.'s haul us to the brig for improper actions."

Ben took in a deep breath and laid his head against January's forehead. "You're right." He straightened in the seat and grasped the steering wheel. "Look across the river to the south. Can you make out the chalk cliff near the grassy area?"

January nodded her head.

"That's Register cliff. That's where we're going next."

"Then why are we sitting on this hill?"

"To get the feel of this small town. The western boundary is the street leading to the mansion. The hills at the north and the river to the south form the other perimeters. If you look at the base of this hill, you see we are sitting at the easternmost point of Garrison.

"It's beautiful the way the sun shines through the fresh leaf-buds on the trees that makes me feel good. It's quite hypnotic." She eased back into the seat and remembering her reluctance about coming to Garrison. That was behind her now. The mansion was nearly completed and now—she was in love with Ben. She wanted to spend every minute with him.

"Do you think we should go over to the cliff when it's this close to sunset?" she asked.

"We should be OK, it's only a few miles over there." He started the vehicle and maneuvered it down the steep hill.

The cliff was much closer than it seemed. They had crossed the river bridge to the south of Garrison and January could see the cliff in the distance. It must have risen over one hundred fifty feet from the grassy bank of the Platte River.

"If you take this dirt path to the west, it leads to the Oregon Trail wagon ruts. But we'll have to save that for another day. It'll be dark by the time we come back this way."

"That's OK. I've seen the ruts already."

He spun around and stared at her. "When?"

She shrugged. "A couple of weeks ago. I was sick of working on the house and decided to take a hike. I tramped all over that historical site!"

She was surprised at all the history surrounding this area and gave her ideas about advertising the bed-and-breakfast. Hopefully, Lionel Danvers would have some useful information for her tomorrow.

January got out of the car in the parking area at the base of the cliff and Ben met her at the front of the vehicle. "Come on." He took her hand. "This is a great place. When I was a kid I spent a lot of hours here. I would pack a lunch and sit in that cave." He gestured with his free hand toward a massive wooden door that covered the entrance to the cave.

"What's in there now?" January asked and skipped toward the door, pulling him along. She put her eye up to the crack between the chalk rock and the wood. "It looks like a tractor is in there. That's really something. A historic place like this being used as a storage garage."

"Come on. Let's look at the names before it gets dark. The old names are on the northern side of the cliff."

They walked on the steep dirt and gravel path past name after name. "Until the fence was built, everyone carved their names in the stone marring the historical names."

"Here they are."

January craned her neck and put her hand on the side of her temple to block the setting sun from fading her vision. "Wow. The name and dates are ancient."

"Yeah. Some of dates and names have washed away over the years. I remember the name of Goodwin Wasburg, July 14, 1829. It was right here." He pointed to a smooth area of rock. "Each year it fades a little more. Look, it's nearly gone."

"Uh-huh, look at this one, G. O. Willard. Boston 1855. That was a long time ago."

Ben came up behind her and gathered her into his arms. "Do you suppose a couple of lovers stood here admiring their work two hundred years ago?"

"I can nearly feel their spirits, alive and loving." January shuddered. Ben might think she was making up the story, but the truth was she really did feel the sensations.

"Let's go. It's getting dark, and you're cold. I felt you shudder."

Once in the car, Ben turned up the heat control.

"Now that it's dark, I want to show you something else. It's extraordinary."

"Oh, and this wasn't?" she jested and slipped into her jacket and shivered against the satin lining.

As they neared the river bridge, Ben turned the blazer into a road that was entirely hidden by the thick grove of brambles that obscured the path. It followed the river.

January wondered if she could see her house from this vantage point, but she doubted it because the trees were so thick. Then, as they approached the knoll of a hill, Ben turned into a path.

Ahead of them stood the grave marker January had seen from the window seat in her bedroom. Quickly, she looked across the river. The mansion was clearly visible. No trees or brush obscured her view.

A faint light shone in the window of her bedroom and framed in the window stood Calico.

CHAPTER 10

January reached out her hand and grasped Ben's arm, her fingers tightened painfully around his wrist. Calico was showing herself with Ben looking on. Or did she know they watching? This side of the house was difficult to see unless you were here at the grave marker.

"Do you see her in the window?" Her voice a mere whisper. She was afraid the sound would carry and alert Calico to their presence even though they were far from the house and near the river.

Ben nodded his head. "I'm starting to believe. But I have no idea why she is here. Do you?"

January stared at the window and watched as Calico faded from view and finally disappeared. "No idea. I am hoping Mr. Danvers will have some answers for us.

"Can I sit in during your interview?"

January hesitated before answering. She was afraid to have him there. She didn't want to feel reserved during the conference with the editor. And then again, she didn't want Ben to feel hurt. Could she accomplish both? "OK...but I want you to sit back and don't ask any questions. If you can do that, I won't mind if you're there."

Ben hesitated to answer, seeming to mull over her ultimatum. Then he nodded his head silently.

"Now, why are we sitting on this knob beside a grave marker?"

"I nearly forgot from the shock of seeing Calico in the window. This is the grave of a pioneer girl. Some people say it is haunted."

Her eyes grew round. "Haven't we had enough weird things happening to us? I can see this stone from the window seat in my bedroom. I had wondered why it was here."

Ben turned in the seat. "Kid's park out here." He gently stroked her cheek, then leaned toward her, kissing her lips briefly. "I felt sure that this ghost would be traced to jealous lovers. But I've changed my mind, I'm a believer now."

"Ummm. It's been a long time since I've parked with a boy. The last time I did this I was a senior. After the prom, we parked at Lookout Mountain where you could see all of Denver from that location." Ben pressed his mouth to hers and stopped her flow of words. She parted her lips and felt herself slip into the dizzy whirlwind of sensation. His kissed deepened and his hands slid between the buttons at the front of her blouse.

Ben pulled away but stayed close, resting his head against her forehead and took her face in his hands. "Y'know, this falling in love stuff is a shock. It wasn't that long ago that I swore I'd never be a relationship another woman and now, here I am."

"Famous last words, huh? I've worn those baggy clothes for years trying to hide my body. I-I didn't want a relationship just because of my body. I thought it would bring out the beast in a man and he'd only want me for sex. Now I realize I was hiding more than my body. I didn't have to deal with a relationship and all that entailed if no one ever got close."

"Don't worry about why I want you because I want all of you, your beautiful brain that came up with the idea to start an Inn, your hands that decorate so beautifully and yes, your body because it makes me feel so loved!"

January was starting to feel embarrassed and self-conscious. "Don't you think we should go home? I'm getting cold."

Ben sat up and reached for the ignition. "Some evening this summer, so you won't get cold, we'll walk around the river. It smells so good in the summer when the Russian Olive trees are in full bloom, and the sound of the water rushing over the rocks is beautiful."

"Umm, I'll look forward to that. But right now, it's been a long day, and I'm exhausted."

Each time January looked at the front of the house, she was aware of the progress Jim made. The freshly painted trim was clear of brush and weeds. The pale yellow, nearly white trim color was almost a duplicate from a picture taken years before that January had found in the antique desk she used for the reception area.

She had poured over the paint samples at the local lumberyard to find a pleasing match for the front door and selected dusty-blue paint for the door, but it hadn't arrived until last week. January was so pleased with the effect. Ordering and waiting was a new experience for January. In the city, if the company didn't have what you wanted, they called across town to one of their other stores and a deliveryman brought the product.

They entered the dark foyer and January flipped the switch that lit the chandelier high above causing the bright light to illuminate all but the corners of the entry.

"I know it's only eight o'clock, but I'm going to my room," January said with a sigh. "This day has been fantastic, but I want to think about things. I really need to be alone for a while."

Ben smiled at her. "I understand. I'll be saying good night, too. I have a few meetings tomorrow, and I'll be leaving for Wyland after the interview."

They walked up the stairway together, and Ben turned to go to his room. He turned toward ther and said, "Jan, I-I hope you aren't upset about, well, you know, making love." He moved closer and pulled her to him. "I truly do love you." He kissed the top of her head and released her and walked to his room.

January stood rooted to the spot and watched him walk away. She knew he loved her, but something was not right. She couldn't pinpoint what the problem was, but she felt something. Sometimes she wished she wasn't psychic and she definitely wished these feelings would skip over her like they had in the past. She didn't want to know things about her own life.

After a long soaking bath, she curled up on the bed with the mystery novel she had been trying to read since coming to Garrison, but her body was so tired from getting the house ready, that she fell asleep after only a few paragraphs. After the events of the day, she was sure she would never be able to sleep, but after few minutes of reading, her eyes closed and she drifted off to sleep with the vision of Ben in her dreams.

JANUARY PULLED THE small weeds from around the tender plants in the flower garden. Since the garden had mysteriously weeded itself, she had taken over the project. The tulips were blooming in profusion against the stone wall the surrounded the garden. An abundance of other spring flowers such as daffodils, crocus, and other unnamed plants grew along the cement paths which lead to the back of the house.

Ben had awakened her at seven and told her that Mr. Danvers had called to tell her he was coming at one o'clock instead of ten. She decided to take advantage of the delay to get some dirty chores done. And Ben rearranged his schedule so he could be with her when Lionel Danvers came for the interview. She had plenty of time to work in the garden and begin cleaning the library because Ben wasn't coming home for lunch until twelve thirty. This would be her most difficult chore. She knew she should wait for help, but she had to begin.

It was only May, but the sun was becoming uncomfortably hot later in the day, so January had risen early to beat the blistering sun. She looked around the garden. Just over a month ago, Ben had upended her over by the lilac bushes and today the bushes were blooming profusely. She smiled and realized their love was growing and blooming just like the flowers. It was fast, but so real and so deep.

January decided to hold off on her shower and had slipped into her holiest jeans and an oversized, bagged-out T-shirt for the gardening. There was no sense getting all cleaned-up just to get muddy in the garden. She was sure to be hot and sweaty after she finished. Since Mrs. Beemer told her about the deaths in the library, January avoided the room. Now she had to clean the library whether she wanted to or not; today was the day.

As she wiped the beads of sweat off her brow with the back of her arm, a clump of dirt dislodged from the small rake she held in her hands. The soil hit her on the forehead and burst into a stream of powder and mixed with the remaining traces of sweat.

January got to her feet and wiped the mud on the seat of her pants. After two hours, she'd had enough gardening for the day and went into the house through the back door and grabbed the lamb's wool duster from the hall closet before heading to the library. The room was dusty, but it wouldn't take much time, maybe an hour to complete the task. Then, she would shower with the knowledge that her house was ready for business. She glanced at her watch, it was only ten o'clock.

She tried hard not to think about what had taken place in this room, but she was sure she sensed a heaviness in the air. The walls wouldn't forget the loss of life, that incident would be imprinted in the atmosphere of this room until the whole house crumbled down on top of it.

January shook herself into focusing on the task at hand. At least the books were behind glass, which should have kept the dust from becoming too thick. She opened a door and wiped the fluff-on-a-stick along the exposed area and her mind filled with images of Ben: His thick, luxuriant brown hair, the curve of his lips. Her breath caught in her throat when she thought of his intoxicating eyes and the way he looked at her continually as they had made love. A small shudder of desire slipped up her spine.

The sound of wheels on the gravel at the front of the mansion brought her out of her daydream.

"There's someone here to see you," Cathy said, standing in the doorway. January couldn't help but notice the smirk on Cathy's face as she turned back into the hallway. The woman and her snarky attitude grated on her nerves. One moment, she was friendly, and the next, she acted as if January was her enemy. What was her problem? At first, January had enjoyed Cathy's company. Jim was so busy that she seldom saw the man. The couple had their own kitchen arranged in their apartment while they waited for the completion of the construction and were self-sufficient. But she had to admit, she did get lonesome at times.

She entered the foyer stopping abruptly as she came face to face with the most beautiful woman she had ever seen. She looked vaguely familiar, but January couldn't place her.

From the front, the woman's hair looked to be a chin-length bob. But when she turned slightly, January could see that the jet-black hair was long, loosely pulled back. A large silk bow that matched her blue, cashmere sweater adorned her hair.

"Hello," January said extending her hand in greeting. She had no idea who the woman was. There was only one word that could describe the stranger's eyes. Intoxicating. She could imagine all the men's hearts that had surrendered to the stare of bright blue with white highlights.

These same eyes stared in disgust at January's hand as if she had extended a three-headed snake. January followed the stranger's gaze down to her side. Dark soil from the garden caked the palms of her hands and nails.

"Oh! I'm sorry," January exclaimed and wiped her hand against the hip of her jeans to remove the soil, then extended it again.

The woman took her hand gingerly as if she was afraid the dirt would rub off. It was only soil, January thought, slightly annoyed. "Nice to meet you," she said, but her nose wrinkled up in distaste. "I'm Audra Lowrey." She whispered her name as if she was uttering a prayer.

"Welcome to Pine Gables." January smiled, gestured toward the drawing room at the left, but Audra looked down her nose at her. Its doors lead to the garden, and the sunlight streaming into the room implied: warmth, friendliness, and security. All the feelings January, at that moment, tried to show in the expression on her face, but she didn't feel that way at all. She hated the feelings this uppity woman brought out in her.

Audra looked around the foyer taking in the expanse of the stairway. "How impressive. You have done phenomenal things to this neglected estate," she said. "It was so depressing before when Ben took me through here." She walked toward the antique desk January planned used as the registration desk.

January froze in her tracks. Audra had been here with Ben? Why hadn't Ben told her this?

"Good Lord! This desk is hand painted. How could you afford, ah where did you buy this? I didn't know there was an antique outlet in this area that could manage to buy such a piece."

January felt her lip begin to curl in a hateful sneer. She knew what Audra actually meant to say. How could January afford this level of refinement? She barely managed to replace the smirk with a sweet smile when Audra turned around and stared at her as she waited for an answer.

January didn't want to discuss the furnishings of the house because it wasn't any of Audra's business. Changing the subject, she asked, "Why are you here?"

The woman didn't answer; she just continued to look at January with a blank expression. There wasn't a crease or line across her smooth forehead.

Audra's superior attitude threatened to break-down January's new, untried self-esteem. She started to feel shy and ordinary again, but straightened her back, took a deep breath. She'd be damned if she'd let this spurious woman cause her to feel this way. She was just as good as this woman. No, actually, January thought she was better, a lot better, because she didn't intentionally plan to hurt people.

"If you don't answer me, you can leave." January spoke, her voice filled with authority that left no doubt that she meant business. It sounded strange to her ears.

"I wanted to see my competition." Audra's chin rose in defiance, and she shot January an icy glare snapping with hatred.

"Competition?"

"Everyone is talking about you and about all the time you've been spending with Ben. I wanted to see you for myself."

"Really? I thought Ben told you to take a hike."

The woman's eyes momentarily widened, but quickly returned to their cold, impassionate gaze. "Oh! Is that what he told you, dear?" Laughter edged her voice. She pulled her leather handbag from her shoulder and flipped open the clasp. Taking a small case from the bag, she withdrew a long, thin cigarette. Placing the white filter to her painted lips, she lit the tip with a jewel-encrusted lighter and took a long draw inhaling the smoke deeply into her body.

"We had a misunderstanding and now, sweetie..." she hissed, her eyes narrowing into snake-like slits. "I want him back."

It was January's turn to be at a loss for words. The combination of the cigarette smoke and Audra's words made her feel light-headed. How could she hope to compete with this woman? She didn't have expensive clothing, and her makeup didn't come from exclusive department stores.

Then she remembered some of the things that Ben told her. All the extravagant adornments meant nothing to him. He said he loved January's natural essence. These thoughts gave her confidence. She actually felt sorry for Audra when she looked at her through Ben's eyes. Fake, pretentious and plastic was the impression Audra made.

January detected a slight tremble as Audra once again raised her hand to inhale the smoke into her lungs. This woman was more upset than she wanted January to believe. Well, well, what are you trying to hide, Audra Lowrey?

"I don't know what I have to do with this. If you want Ben back, you'd better speak to him directly." January's voice grew stronger as she gained control of the conversation. January filled with optimism. She was so pleased that she was holding her own against someone that continually got their own way.

Unable to upset January, Audra began to pace the entry. "I don't know why Ben hasn't yet sold this estate to the Willis Company. When you arrived, the contract was nearing completion. All he needed was your signature. If you hadn't interfered, they would have their people in place by now, and Ben and I would be on our honeymoon!" Audra's words spun through January's head. Could it be possible Audra was lying in an attempt to rattle her nerves? Ben would clear this up.

The thick smoke that swirled through the foyer reminded her she needed to post No Smoking signs on each floor. The antiques could be ruined by hot ashes and the oily film produced by the smoke.

"You, Audra, are not welcome here. Get out of my house," January whispered to her uninvited guest. The smell of the cigarette smoke made her feel nauseated.

Audra tossed her head and raised her chin defiantly as she walked to the door. "You're out of your league, little girl. Why don't you go back to your mundane existence of dumping bedpans and get lost in the city? Ben's mine and I will have him." With that, she flung open the door and marched out.

January stood on the porch and watched Audra drive away, then she dropped onto the step. What was happening to her emotions? First, she was high, her heart soaring with the birds out in the garden, then Audra walks into the house causing her feelings to plummet. Sitting there, she began to lose what little grip on confidence she had gained since living in Wyoming.

Through tear-filled eyes, she walked back inside the house and found her way to the kitchen and to the cabinet where she kept a bottle of pain reliever. Her head was pounding as she opened the bottle, removed two white tablets and dropped the bitter things onto her tongue then washed them down with the icy well water. Leaning against the cabinet, January realized her headache was caused by the anger pulsing through her body. Anger at Audra, anger at possibly being duped by Ben and anger at herself for trusting Ben in the first place. She wanted to believe Ben loved her, but it was so maddening when her old insecurities reared their ugly heads. She looked at her watch. Eleven thirty! As she walked through the dining room, she caught a glimpse of herself in the mirror. She looked terrible. Her hair hung in greasy strands and there was a dirty streak across her cheek where she'd wiped away a trickle of sweat. No wonder Audra had appeared so self-assured. Audra must be laughing her head off after seeing her competition. That bitch! She could bet the exquisite woman wondered about Ben's sanity after seeing January looking so pathetic. Audra's words spun in January's mind.

By the time January stepped out into the hallway, clean and tidy, she was confused, upset and downright livid. There was just enough time to clean up before Ben came for lunch. Why she cared what she looked like was a wonder with the awful thoughts and emotions spinning through her. She moved slowly up the steps headed for her room.

January entered the kitchen after her bath and found Cathy eating a sandwich. "Hi," Cathy said shyly. "I've been hidin' back here. I'm sorry 'bout earlier. I just get so mad when I have to stop workin' to answer that damn door! Oh, and Ben called, he's going to be a few minutes late."

"Well great! Mr. Danvers rescheduled as well."

Cathy slumped in the chair.

"What's the matter with you, Cathy?"

"I'm beat. All this work is getting to me."

"Is that all?"

"I guess so," she said quietly, "I only have enough energy to tackle one thing at a time."

January shook her head. "No, Cathy, I think we're going to need more help. Starting the first week in June, we'll have customers. How can I help ease the load on you?"

Cathy stared at January. "You mean it?"

"Yes. There is too much work to do. I never dreamed this inn would take off so quickly."

Cathy pushed her sandwich away. "I think we've got the mansion ready, but we forgot about who was going to do all this work. Jim will be busy with the grounds and maintenance. I like puttering around doing the house cleaning. You manage the money, keep everyone on track. We need a cook, someone to do the laundry and a host or hostess."

"You're right, and I feel terrible for not thinking this through. Write down every chore you think of, and we'll start making job descriptions." The eerie tones of the doorbell rang through the house ending their conversation.

"Go ahead with your lunch, I'll answer the door." She looked at her watch, it was nearly one. "It's probably Mr. Danvers." She knew it couldn't be Ben because he just entered without fanfare. January rushed out of the swinging door and scurried through the dining room as the bell rang again. Cathy was right. They could use someone just to greet guests!

She opened the door, and Lionel Danvers stood there waiting for her. His clothing stretched and bagged in the warm afternoon sun, and he had a camera bag slung over his shoulder.

"I'm sorry I had to postpone earlier," Mr. Danvers apologized. "And I only have an hour to spend with you now."

"Oh, I was going to show you through the house." Disappointment edged her voice.

"Let's do it quickly." He brusquely entered the foyer. "We can talk while you give me the tour." He opened his leather bag and removed a camera and a notepad then tossed the bag onto the desk.

"Right this way. Let's start in the drawing room."

Forty-five minutes later, they reentered the foyer from the back hall. "What about room rates? Will it be..." The telephone interrupted Mr. Danvers question.

"Excuse me a moment," she said as she stood, then walked to the small table across the room that held the old, black phone with a rotary dial in the middle. January answered, "Pine Gables, may I help you?"

"Jan? Ben asked.

"Just a minute." She cradled the receiver in the crook of her neck covering the mouthpiece and asked Mr. Danvers, "Would you excuse me for a moment? I have to take this call."

He nodded. "I'll go in the drawing room."

"Thanks." She smiled sincerely at him. "I'll only be a moment."

When Lionel Danvers closed the doors, she spoke. "Ben, where are you?"

"Sorry, I'm late. I had a snag in the closing. The title insurance wasn't ready, and we had to wait for that. Is Danvers there?"

"Yes. He can't stay long, so I need to make this call quick."

"Well, I wanted to let you know that I won't be home until...oh, let's say six. That should be safe."

Her heart softened as she talked to him, but she was damned angry with him. She had trusted him, but then Audra had come to the house and shaken her confidence.

She went to the drawing room and situated herself in a straight chair across from the editor.

"January, have you seen any more bodies lying around the ballroom?"

She flushed. Why did it have to sound so neurotic when the newspaperman asked the question? "No. Nothing like that. I think fatigue had a large hand in that."

"That's understandable. It looks like you've spent a lot of hours working on the house."

"Is there any way you can downplay this?"

Nodding, he smiled and said, "I think it can be arranged."

"I've been so excited to talk to you. Have you found any archived articles about this house or the people that lived here?"

Mr. Danvers shook his head. "I've looked through the papers, and I haven't found one article."

She slumped the chair. "I was afraid of that. Did you get my message yesterday?"

The editor dropped his gaze to the floor. "No. I've been busy. There must be twenty messages on my phone. What did you have to tell me?"

January told him about Mrs. Beemer. "She thought it happened in the mid eighties."

Mr. Danvers twisted his large mustache as he contemplated her request. "I have to go back to Wyland when I leave here. I'll look through everything I have stored in the back room. I was looking fifty years before that date!"

"I'm sorry, I must be keeping your from your work." January rose from the chair, and he mimicked her movement.

As they walked toward the door he said, "I've enjoyed meeting you and seeing this wonderful mansion. I'll be back. I really want to see the rest of the property. Say, do you want to proof the article before I go to print?" Danvers asked before he stepped out the door.

"I can do that?"

"Sure."

"I want to see how you sidestepped the ballroom incident."

He snapped a picture of January as she stood in the doorway. "I won't do you any harm. Good luck with your project. It looks like you're on the way to success."

BEN WALKED INTO THE foyer promptly at six o'clock. Instinctively, he knew something was wrong. "January, I'm here," he called into the dining room. Silence answered his call. January was nowhere to be found. Where the heck could she be? If he remembered correctly, they had a dinner date. He planned to fix them a special, romantic meal and he smiled thinking of her. She had been so animated early that morning. She had many plans for the day, and her green eyes had glistened and danced. Then when he canceled the meeting with Danvers she seemed somewhat annoyed, or was there more to it?

An aroma floated from the area of the kitchen. He wanted to drink in her beauty and kiss her sweet lips, that was all he needed.

Walking into the kitchen, he found January sitting at the small rustic table. Her eyes were scrunched-up causing lines and deep creases to spread across her usually smooth forehead. Her fingertips moved in circles at her temples.

"Are you all right?" Ben rushed to her side and dropped down on one knee. His heart hammered in his chest, afraid to hear her reply.

"No-o-o-o. You're home already?"

He looked into her eyes and found them cloudy and red-rimmed. "You've been crying, what's the matter?"

She pulled her hands away from her face, and he watched as her beautiful face morphed into a mask of hostility and rage. The anger he found there was strong and powerful. What had he done? He knew she had felt some embarrassment about the escalation of their relationship, but that couldn't have turned into this, could it?

"Nothing's the matter! I look like this all the time." She stood, glaring at him.

Why wouldn't she talk logically to him? Apprehension skittered up his spine and tightened his throat, he swallowed with difficulty. Trying to change the subject he asked, "Uh, Jan, I thought I was making dinner for us tonight?"

Turning her back on him, she walked to the sink and filled a tumbler with water. A pregnant silence filled the room.

What had happened to her?

"Cathy re-heated some stew. You can have it any time you want."

He had to strain to hear her words. "But I thought..."

"... that I was sharing a romantic dinner with you?"

"Well, I changed my mind."

With that, she walked from the room and left him standing alone in the middle of the kitchen. His jaw fell slack. He closed his open mouth so quickly that his teeth snapped together with a sharp clack. This felt like he had walked into the middle of a movie not knowing the plot or the characters. A frightening thought struck him. Was she possessed? Had the ghost's spirit crawled into January?

What a ridiculous thought! Fatigue permeated his body and anger zipped through his mind like lightning in a summer thunderstorm. Nothing, absolutely nothing made him angrier than being ignored. He wouldn't play games with her, not this kind anyway.

He took down a bowl from the cupboard and ladled in the thick stew. This was not how he had imagined the evening. It wasn't like he had a lot of dates.

Audra had been the first woman he had gone out with for several months. The selection of single women in this area was thin. He found most of them were looking for the perfect husband and he wasn't ready to be offered on the auction block, just yet. He couldn't pinpoint when his relationship with Audra had escalated to engagement.

His relationship with January was different. He wanted to consume her, body and soul. He wanted to spend every moment with her. And yes, he just might be ready to commit to her.

Lifting the white ceramic handle on the roll-top breadbox, he grasped a loaf of freshly baked bread and carried it to the table. He had just spooned stew into his mouth when January reentered the room. She walked stiffly to the range and filled her bowl. He watched her jerky movements over the top of his glasses.

She said nothing as she sat down across from him. Stony silence filled the room.

"I closed on the Webb ranch today."

She said nothing in return.

"It was quite a lot easier than the last ranch sale I had. That one lasted for weeks."

January continued to eat and ignored him as if he wasn't in the room.

Her snub pushed him over the edge. Ben slammed his spoon into the bowl causing a loud clatter and bits of tomato and onion flew about the table.

January didn't react to the sound.

"January, I've had enough!" Why was she doing this? Had she lost her mind? "What the hell is the matter with you?" Still, she didn't answer.

"January, answer me right now!" Ben felt anger flush his face.

She raised her gaze and her upper lip curled in an ugly sneer. "Leave me alone. I want you to pack up and go. I don't need your protection. I don't need or want you here!"

Throwing her napkin onto the dirty table, she pushed back her chair so violently that it toppled with a clatter against the stone floor as she attempted to flee.

"You aren't going anywhere and neither am I. I want an answer to my questions." He caught her arm just as she started to push open the door. His voice shook with emotion. "The more questions I ask, the touchier you get. I'm only asking you one more time, what's going on?"

"Yeah, as if you don't know. I suspect Audra has already talked to you and convinced you to go back to her."

Ben heart sank to his toes. What was she talking about? "I don't understand."

"Audra was here, Ben. She told me all about your plans to sell this property and how I messed-up your scheme."

"No way!"

"I don't want to hear your excuses. I feel lied to. You used me! You didn't make love to me because you loved me, you did it for your big commission, you did it for money."

"That's enough!" Ben shouted. "Yes, I was going to sell the estate, you know that, I told you all about it. Then you came along with all of your hopes and dreams wrapped up in this house. I fell in love with you, not money. Don't you ever forget that. For God's sake, Jan, I'm in love with you!"

January stared at him, her eyes growing wide. His admission of love finally had meaning. Until that moment, she realized she had doubts about his love buried deep in her heart. She hadn't believed him. She dropped into the chair. Tears welled in her eyes. "But Audra wants you back."

"So what? Don't I have something to say about it? She isn't going to get me back because she never really had me. All the time we were together, I felt uneasy about our relationship. She wanted things that didn't interest me in the least. So how can she expect to get back what she never had?" Ben ran his fingers through his hair in frustration.

"Ben, what are we going to do? Audra is going to make a lot of trouble for us."

"She'll do nothing of the sort." He stomped from the room, walked to the foyer, and grabbed his coat from the back of the chair where he had tossed it when he entered the house earlier.

"Ben, please..." January clutched at his arm trying to change his course, but she was too small to make much difference. His size overwhelmed her. "She'll just become more vicious!"

His body seemed to collapse as the anger subsided. Ben bent down and brushed his lips against hers. "I have to try and do something even if it is wrong. You can understand that, can't you?"

January nodded sadly. "I guess all I can say is—good luck—and that I'm sorry. I'd been telling myself all day to give you a chance to defend yourself, I guess as the day wore on, I lost control. I don't want to lose you, Ben. I-I l-love you, too."

January looked so tired, and he regretted Audra hurting her this way. Now was the time to confront that vindictive woman. He didn't want to wait until his anger subsided. Leaning down, he kissed January's lips. "I'll see you in a while. I love you so much. I hate to leave you, but I must have this out with Audra."

He stepped out on the porch and pulled the door shut behind him. She had said she loved him. That was all that he needed to hear. Surely, Audra didn't want him under these circumstances.

As he put the key in the ignition, his pager went off. So much for talking to Audra in the heat of anger.

THE LIGHTS WERE ON at Audra's condo. Ben steered his vehicle into the driveway and screeched to a stop. Damn, that woman infuriated him. She sure had a lot of nerve saying those hurtful things to January. Well, she was going to hear about it! It sure wasn't going to be what she had hoped for. Wanted him back, indeed!

He wished he could have confronted Audra when his anger was hot, but he'd been called to the EMT barn just as he left January. One of the local kids had fallen and cut a gash in her head, more blood than damage really. He had butterflied the cut and her parents took her on to the emergency room over in Wyland.

He pushed the doorbell several times and could hear the bell ringing inside the apartment along with Audra's feminine voice calling for him to wait a moment.

His heart thundered with anger. He couldn't remember ever being so mad at anyone.

Audra opened the door a crack, and when she saw him, she threw the door open fully. "What a nice surprise! Come in, come in."

"I want to talk to you, lady. Why did you go and upset January? Didn't you realize I had turned down the offer to let Jan have a go with the Inn?" His words rushed out not giving her a chance to answer.

"Oh, it's Jan now, is it? How cozy," Audra spat with a venom-filled sharpness. She walked up the stairs to the living room and draped herself across a plush overstuffed chair.

Ben followed her and stood over her as she lounged easily. It was like he was looking at her for the first time. She was beautiful, but hard at the same time.

"Audra, I'm in love with Jan. Why did you tell her that you wanted me back?"

She raised her mascara-rimmed eyes and stared at him. She licked her lips and ran her hands down the inside seams of her tight black jeans. "Because, darling, I do want you."

Ben shook his head in disgust. She stood, and leaned into his body. She ran her hands up his chest and pressed her thin body against his.

He dug his fingers into her shoulders and pushed her away.

"I can see we need to talk," Audra whispered. "I'll make a pot of tea."

"That's not necessary. I..." Ben began, but Audra walked into the kitchen as if she hadn't heard a thing he said.

He dropped onto the pillowy couch to wait for her return. If Audra didn't want to hear, she easily avoided listening. How in the world had he thought he cared for such a selfish woman?

Audra reentered the room with a ceramic tea service sitting on a large tray. She placed it in the middle of the glass table. "Here you go, darling." She handed him a steaming cup of tea. "It's so hot I poured them in the kitchen so they would cool slightly."

Taking her cup from the tray, she settled herself in the chair directly across from Ben. She tucked her jeans-clad leg under her and sipped at the rich coffee. "Okay, talk."

Ben shook his head. "Don't be hostile, Audra. I-I came to tell you face-to-face that I'm in love with January. As a matter of fact, I'm going to ask her to marry me. That eliminates any possibility of our relationship continuing."

Audra's face paled and he caught a sparkling glimmer of tears in her eyes before she turned her head. A wall of straight black hair hid the tears from his line of vision.

"I don't think it will work that way. No, you won't have her." The words were spoken in a whispered monotone. "I know something you don't."

Ben's head began to swim and the room looked like it was under water. All the colors blended together. He didn't feel well at all. "Umm...Audra what are you talking about."

Audra stood and went to Ben's side and sat near him. Taking his hand, she continued. "Ben, Ben, Ben, you can't marry January."

"What?"

"No," she whispered into his ear. "I've researched this matter thoroughly. January is your sister."

Her words rang in his ears as he fell over on his side. "NO! She can't be! Wh-what did you d-do to me?" It was an effort to get the words from his flaccid lips.

Audra kissed him on the cheek. "Go to sleep, darling. I only gave you a couple of sleeping pills. Tomorrow morning it will all be over. She will be eliminated from our lives. I know you want it that way, don't you?"

That was the last thing he heard before the oppressive fatigue crashed over him like a tall ocean wave.

CHAPTER 11

January's life was a mess. Is this what happens when you lack experience in matters of the heart? Her emotions were erratic. She leaned against the front door; Ben's angry face was etched in her memory. How could she claim to love him, then immediately jump to the wrong conclusion when vindictive Audra appeared on the scene? But she knew that she loved him and bashing herself for getting angry with him was just grasping at something that would give her some piece of mind and not make her feel so moronic.

Something bothered her, nagged at the back of her mind. Something was wrong. She paced the room as fear covered her shoulders like a cape.

She couldn't think anymore. She felt disassociated from the real world and wanted to drown her hands in soapy dishwater, there was nothing more real than washing dishes. Cathy and Jim had the night off and if Cathy came to work in the morning and found the kitchen in shambles...well, January didn't want that to happen. They had made so much progress today.

Excitement flooded through her. She really was opening her own business. Her dream was at hand.

Washing dishes was therapeutic. It calmed her nerves and offered her a clean palate for reflection. Was Ben with Audra right now? Had Audra's charm captivated him? Stop it! January reprimand herself for thinking about that. As angry as Ben was when he left, she doubted he would find Audra alluring.

After she dried and put the dishes away, January rambled around the house aimlessly. Something was bothering her, but she couldn't find the problem. She dimmed the lights in the drawing room, sat in her favorite chair and relaxed, willing each muscle to release its pent-up tension. This form of relaxation usually triggered a psychic response, but nothing happened. The lack of reaction felt strange. All these years she had forced herself not to use her psychic abilities, and then this one time when she needed it, it wasn't there for her.

She had to do something to calm her nervousness. Stay busy, she told herself. She hadn't finished cleaning the library today, and she couldn't think of one reason why she shouldn't do just that.

Switching on the light, the fixture glowed dimly in the center of the high ceiling. Apparently, it hadn't been cleaned all the time that the house was closed. Even at this distance, intricate spider webs crammed the space between the glass and the ceiling, which reduced the output of light. The only positive thing the room had going for it was that the books were behind glass doors. At least, light filtered into the room through the age thinned draperies. It was seven o'clock and the recent change to daylight-saving time made the evening light last much longer.

January pushed back the curtain and looked out onto the patio and anticipated the long, hot summer evenings that she would spend outdoors with inn guests. She planned to serve her mother's special recipe of homemade lemonade in the tall crystal glasses she found stored in the attic. In the back of a kitchen drawer, she found frosted glass stir rods to use with the flutes. Every little item she uncovered brought a flood of ideas.

Dropping the dusty material she spoke out loud, "If I don't get this house finished I won't have a single customer!" A distant rumble caught her attention. She stepped into the hallway and found a west-facing window and looked into the sky. Earlier, she had noticed that Laramie Peak had trapped a thick band of clouds. Now, the tall peak couldn't hold the energy back and a dark, ominous thunderhead pulled from its grasp and soared in the evening sky. She loved the power and beauty of a thunderstorm. Excitement and anticipation of the season's first storm skittered through her veins.

She walked back to the library, her sandals clapping against her naked feet echoed in the hallway. Her duster was still lying on the desk where she had placed it earlier and she pulled out a straight-back chair and climbed on it to try and reach the light fixture.

A faint whispering laugh echoed through the dark paneled room. January stepped down from the chair and whirled in a circle looking for the source. "Calico...you shouldn't frightened me like that when I'm in such a dangerous position! Why don't you help me out and whisk away all this dust like you cleaned the flower garden?"

Suddenly, a wispy column of smoke formed near the massive wooden desk. The apparition swayed back and forth over the top of the desk as if calling to her.

The last time Calico had done this, January had followed her direction and ended up in the ballroom. She wasn't so sure she was going to do the ghosts bidding this time. The hypnotic effect of Calico's swaying movement confused her momentarily. January's feet seemed to move toward the spirit of their own accord. She tried to gain control, but she felt like a speck of lint caught in the powerful whirlpool of spiraling water as it was pulled closer and closer to the drain.

By the time January touched the desk, the delicate strands of smoke had disappeared leaving her alone in the room once again. Her knees knocked together violently and she pulled the leather-covered desk chair under her to keep her from falling. She knew the ghost wanted to tell her something. This feeling was elusive as the flimsy form Calico had used. Were her extrasensory gifts the root of this problem? Just what was Calico trying to tell her?

Night fell and shrouded the room in a blanket of darkness as January sat at the desk lost in thought. Not even the sharp cracks of lightening penetrated her stupor. Her thoughts were a jumble. Pictures of Ben entwined with the image of Audra. What was happening to her? She didn't know how to interpret this vision. She was too close to unravel the meaning. Was Ben in Audra's arms while she was sat alone in this dusty room with only a long-dead ghost for company?

If she didn't have such a strong desire to make a success of this business, she'd go home to her family. It had been months since she found out she was adopted and she had never felt so close to her parents. They would have told her the truth if they had been allowed, but the terms of the adoption prohibited that.

"Stop it!" she shouted, breaking through the trance-like daze. Her voice seemed hollow and thin. Ghosts and Ben's ex-fiancée were getting to her. She needed to work, she needed to distance herself from that damned image that played in her mind. She shuddered violently. Ben should have been back by now!

She stood on the chair, but she couldn't reach the cobwebs. At least the library was close to the kitchen. She wouldn't have to drag her ladder, vacuum and cleaners very far. The equipment was new, but it had taken a real beating to whip this house into a clean shape.

To keep the vacuum bag in place, she had wrapped a strip of duct tape around the body of the machine. At least the darn thing had quit dropping open as she used it. Once, she was nearly finished cleaning a bedroom when the door opened and the dirt-filled bag fell out. The huge cloud of dust that settled over the room had been enough to bring her to tears and along with it, the determination to fix the problem.

After cleaning the light, corners, and windowsills, she tackled the books thinking they would be the easiest chore. Wrong. She had to discard the duster and use the soft-bristle brush on the end of the vacuum cleaner hose, delicately eliminating the thick dust that filled the recessed area at the top of the book.

The process would be slow at best. Up and down the ladder she went. The pile of cleaned books grew in the corner of the room.

What a mess!

She hadn't realized the enormity of this project. Not only were the books dirty, but the shelves were also sticky and dirt covered. Wiping across a shelf above eye level something dislodged and it produced a metallic clattering as it hit the floor.

She sighed with fatigue not wanting to navigate the ladder any more than was necessary. Her legs felt heavy and throbbed with pain as she moved down the ladder. And she had thought she was in good shape!

January looked around the floor and finally spotted a small brass key near the edge of the bookcase. She squatted slowly and flipped the key on edge to pick it up. As she touched the metal, psychic pictures started their unrelenting kaleidoscope behind her eyes sweeping her away to another dimension; a place where she could see behind the thin veil that separated reality and the future. Instinctively, January knew this was a full-blown vision. She watched herself walk toward the desk, and as she placed the key in a lock, it turned.

As suddenly as the vision had begun, January snapped back to reality with a jolt, a reaction so strong, she cratered to the floor. Most of the time the return trip was gentle, but this time was different, not only was the image different, so was the completion. The clarity astounded her. Shaking her head, she stared at the key. Was this what Calico was trying to tell her?

Taking a deep breath, she steadied herself and walked to the desk. Just as in her 'dream' the key turned. But unlike her vision, a drawer opened.

It was empty.

Well, this is really interesting. Why the image in the first place? Ever since she had stepped to this house, her psychic ability seemed bent. This messed-up vision proved it.

"I don't understand!" In frustration and annoyance, January slammed her hand down on the open drawer and broke into silent tears. From behind her, she perceived an audible creaking groan. Her back became rigid and inflexible as frozen waves of fear undulated up her spine.

Reluctantly, January turned. The end section of the bookcase swung out from the wall and revealed another room positioned behind the shelving.

January stood and slowly made her way to the door and entered the dark room feeling along the cold wall until her fingers touched a switch protruding into the room. She flipped the button into the on position and the area flooded with soft yellow light from a small lamp atop a small desk.

The room was small, the length of the shelves and and not too deep. Why would someone build the room this way? Was it a secret room or was it made for quiet and privacy? This would be a wonderful place for her office. At one time she had considered using the library as her office, but that was before she saw this new space and experienced the feelings it evoked. It would offer the guests an opportunity to enjoy many of the classics from the shelves of the library if it weren't here office.

Possibly, she'd add a door opening onto the patio. It would do the trick. A French door would let in light and serve as another way into the room if the library was in use. That way, the borders could enjoy the library without January disturbing them. Right now her ledgers and numerous letters were piled in her bedroom.

January walked into the room and stepped onto an old braided rug. The room looked cozy and quaint—feminine, in fact. A small settee and little end table filled one side of the room, and a desk and ladder-back chair sat against the far wall.

This must have been someone's favorite room. There were numerous hardcover journals on the desk and an old cigar box.

She dusted the seat off with her hand and in a quick movement, slapped her hands together to remove the dust balls. All those dusty books in the main library were depressing, but exploring a secret room sounded like fun. Old houses were so impressive. Living in Denver, she looked forward to weekly estate auctions. She poured over the Rocky Mountain News to decide which auctions to attend. She and Brandy, a friend from work, set out each Saturday to visit as many estates as time and their money would allow.

As a result, January's apartment in Denver overflowed with unique treasures. She couldn't afford to buy the expensive antique furniture, but she had a fondness for offbeat trinkets, pillows, all those items that no one was interested in buying.

The first journal she leafed through appeared to have been written by a young girl. Finally, the last book in the collection caught her interest.

February 14 Valentine's Day

I waited for Cal in the carriage house. He insisted I be there, but he didn't show up. I sold my jewelry and told Xander I lost it. I'm sure he didn't believe me. Especially since I was wearing the antique Cameo necklace that grandmother Call gave me. Well...I had to do something. Cal insisted I pay him money and Xander must never find out that baby Alexis is Cal Reeder's daughter.

As she began to read her heart went out to the tormented journal writer.

March 2. Everything is fine. Cal hasn't been around for over two weeks. This nightmare is finished.

May 1. Baby Alexis is four months old. She is so adorable. My little towhead. I'm only afraid Xander will guess her parentage if Cal comes around. She has his almond-shaped green eyes. I love our small family, but it's so difficult taking care of two children. Cameron, Alexander's little cutie is a handful. At two-years-old, he is into everything. I feel so sorry for him. I think he still misses his mommy. It makes me wonder why God takes away someone so young, someone that has so much to live for.

July 19. He's back. Now, he wants an incredible amount. I don't know what to do.

January flipped the pages looking for the outcome of this deception. She finally found what she was looking for near the back of the journal. It was the last entry. God! Was this the date in 1988? Could Alice Beemer have been this far off? January wondered.

September 27. I did it. Thank God, Alexander was away. I called his accountant and pretended my husband needed a large sum of money, and he gave me a cashier's check. I hope Cal will be satisfied with the funds and the assignment of rights to all my movies. They should bring an extraordinary sum over the years. My freedom is all I want. I will only have a short time to worry. I'm meeting Cal at the carriage house. I want this ordeal finished once and for all. It will be completed. He has to free me from this. If not, I'll rely on my small pistol in my coat pocket

January's heart went out to the woman. How had she become involved with such a man? She sighed, thinking that human relationships were difficult to understand at best.

She would have to ask Mr. Danvers to look up these dates. Miranda sounded desperate. Her husband must have found out about her affair and killed her, then himself.

January glanced around the room. This must have been the woman's sanctuary. So why were these journals still here? She stacked the books in a neat pile on top of the dusty desk and reached for the cigar box. Curled, yellow newspaper clippings filled the box. They crackled as she unfurled the old paper. Ever so delicately, she arranged them across the desk.

The first clipping showed a picture of Alexander and Miranda Ford as they entered the ballroom on the third floor of the mansion.

It was dated February 14, 1988.

Was this the dance Mrs. Beemer attended? The only way to describe Miranda was beautiful. The black and white photograph was yellowed, but January could tell she had very light hair that hung to her waist. Alexander looked much older than his wife, but she was turned toward him and gave him a look of adoration. That made January smile.

They looked so happy together. So what had happened to their relationship? Miranda's journal told a story of deception and lies. And Mrs. Beemer's tale of murder and suicide chilled her to the depths of her soul.

She continued looking through the clippings. Older articles displayed images of Miranda in her role of movie celebrity. The reviews she read sounded terrific. How sad. The young woman had everything going for her, a dream profession, and adoring husband.

The telephone interrupted January's research. She raced through the hallway and skidded to a stop at her desk in the foyer hoping to hear Ben's voice on the other end of the line.

"Hello?" She was out of breath and panting

"Miss Mohr?"

"Yes?"

"This is Lionel Danvers. I-I have some information for you. Your informant was nearly right but the date..."

"...September 1988?"

"Why, yes. Have you found something yourself?"

January pulled a chair from under the table and sat. "Mr. Danvers, I think you had better tell me what you have and I'll see how my information fits in with it."

"I quite agree. In an article dated September 27, 1988, Alexander Ford murdered his wife, then shot himself. I have the newspapers and I can bring them by tomorrow."

"I'd appreciate that. I've found some journals written by Miranda Ford, it you'd be interested, you could look through them."

Mr. Danvers was quiet for a moment. "January, you've told me you're adopted and I've heard about the legacy of the mansion, but I-I've been hearing rumors that you and...Ben. That you're an, item."

"What does that have to do with this?" She asked. Her voice was thin and tight with emotion.

"Well, the Ford's had two children. The mister had a two-year-old son from a previous marriage, then he and the misses had a baby daughter. I thought, well, you can see what it looks like. Could you and Mr. Cottier be siblings?"

A ringing in her ears made her feel dizzy and disoriented. She closed her eyes momentarily to regain her balance. She and Ben? Brother and sister? The thought never had formed in her mind, thank God. "No! Absolutely not. I've just read the journals. Miranda was being blackmailed. Alexander Ford was not the daughter's father!"

"Good Lord! And I thought nothing of interest ever took place in this little town. Can I come by around eight o'clock in the morning before I open the office? Those journals sound quite interesting."

"I'll be here, but give me a little time to get to the door, okay?" She laughed gaily, happy and excited that the mysterious legacy was nearing the end. "By the way, I do think that Ben and I are the children in those articles. See you tomorrow."

She hung up the old black rotary-dial phone.

January hurried back into the hidden room and snatched the journals from the top of the desk. Miranda had written about her baby! January was both ecstatic and down-hearted to think she may be reading memoirs written by her biological mother. She opened the last journal and ran her finger down the entries.

Here!

The May first entry; baby Alexis' was four months old that day. January counted back. The baby was born January 1, 1988. That was her birth date. My God, she was that baby produced by Miranda Call-Ford and Cal Reeder.

She ran her hand through her hair and groaned. It made sense. She and Ben were involved in this estate for some reason. Tomorrow, she and Ben could go to the courthouse in Wyland and explore the old records.

It was dark now, and the small desk lamp didn't do much for illuminating the room. She gathered up the clipping and replaced them in the cigar box and placed it on the stack of journals. When Ben returned, they could put their heads together and possibly come up with some answers. When she thought of Ben, the oddest sensation whirled in the pit of her stomach.

January stood and slid the chair back under the desk. She had to locate Audra's house and find Ben. Something was wrong. Very wrong.

A metallic click reverberated through the room. January spun around. Her mouth fell open.

"I've search this entire house from top to bottom. How nice of you to find the journals for me.

BEN'S EYES FELT HEAVY as rocks, and his head pounded dreadfully. What was the matter with him? He struggled to sit up, but his body felt out-of-control. He had to wake up. There was something important he had to do, but the thick fog threatened to obliterate his thoughts.

January! Audra was going to hurt her! He had to do something. It took all of his will power to command his stone-like arm to move. A slight twitch in his index finger was all he could muster. How long had he been out while January was in danger? The wave of darkness overtook him once again and he drifted away with the feeling. In his mind, he was calling to her, calling her name.

"HAND ME THE JOURNALS," Audra voice was rough with hatred. It sounded flat and off-key. Her expression was one of cold loathing.

January blinked, clearly shocked. "W-Why? Why are you doing this?" Nothing in Audra's manner earlier had given January any indication that the woman was menacing. But there was no doubt in January's mind that the woman holding the gun on her was very dangerous indeed.

"If you want to know, start walking to the attic. I'll tell you there." She motioned with the pistol and stepped aside to allow January out the door.

January stood her ground. Now that she was in control of her life, she wasn't letting anyone take it from her without a fight. Then, January flew through the doorway and bounced off the hallway wall. She tried to focus her eyes, but the room spun in circles. Audra had just flung her across the room. Suddenly, fear filled her.

"Get up!" Audra screamed. Then, very calmly, she said, "I never suspected this room was hiding behind the bookshelves. Whoever built this house did an excellent job of hiding this chamber."

January struggled to her feet, leaning against the wall for support. Calico! Help me. The words screamed through her mind. Audra pushed her out into the foyer and over to the stairway. Suddenly, January could faintly smell the scent of lilacs, but the window at the head of the stairs was open, and the fragrance could be originating from the lilac bushes that were in full-bloom outside.

The stairway leading to the upper floors look dark and foreboding. She had been so engrossed with the journals that she hadn't switched on any lights in the house. She wanted to stay on the main floor so that Ben would be able to find her when he came in. Suddenly, she shuddered as a tremor of apprehension crawled up her backbone. Ben! What had Audra done to him?

"What did you do to Ben?"

Audra ignored her question.

As Audra propelled her up the staircase, the temperature began to drop. Calico was near. The smell of lilac became more intense and was so impenetrable it felt like a wall of odor.

Audra gagged, then gulped for air. "What is that horrible smell?"

Taking advantage of Audra's momentary lapse, January spun around. "Where's Ben?" she shouted. "He went to your apartment hours ago." January flung her arm out to push the woman down the stairs, but Audra stepped to the side in anticipation of January's futile attempt.

"Oh, poor, poor thing. You're so concerned about him aren't you, dear?" she spat. "Don't worry about him. He's all right. I gave him enough sleeping pills to keep him under for hours. Now, you start walking toward that attic."

January climbed a few stairs, but her legs felt like wood and wouldn't react. They didn't want to move or hold her weight. She stumbled and fell on a wooden step, her shin throbbed painfully where the bone had come in contact with the sharp edge of the stair.

"Get up!" Audra screamed, yanking January's hair as she pulled her to her feet. January could see Audra's eyes. They were glassy with insanity.

Pushing with both of her hands January righted herself and continued the trek toward her captor's destination. As they walked across the hallway on the second floor, she glimpsed Calico's form. The ghost was watching over her, and this made her feel brave. At least she wasn't alone!

"Audra. Y-You'll never get away with this. Let me go." January rationalized.

The only response was a brutal shove in the middle of her back.

"Shut up or I'll shoot you."

January didn't doubt that for Audra's voice was cold and heartless, and she picked up her pace, entering the dark attic in only a few moments.

Entering the shadowy room, January reached out and pulled a string hanging in front of her face only inches from her nose. The light cast a sickly yellow glow over the dusty items stored in the room.

"Walk over to the window." Audra said, pointing with the nose of the gun. "You are going to commit suicide."

"No!" January's mind spun looking for a way out of the situation. She prayed Calico would help her somehow.

"So, should I shoot you?" She asked, smiling. "I would rather you jumped. A bullet through your brain would make such a mess and I have to live in this house for the rest of my life. I don't want that picture in my mind every time I come up here."

January's body began a violent tremble. So much for being brave with a ghost on your side. She was sure any moment now, that she would be joining Calico in the spirit world. If Audra was so confident that she would be the next mistress of the manor, then she had better be prepared to deal with two ghosts. January planned on driving Audra more insane than she was at this moment.

Audra narrowed her eyes and stared at January. "There is a suicide note on the table by the window. I used your computer to compose the letter. All that is left is for you to do is sign it. Do it, now!"

January shook her head. She had to think of something to save herself, fast. Calico, help me, tell me what to do! she pleaded to the ghost. But nothing changed.

"Audra. Don't you think it's fair to tell me what this is about before you kill me? You can have Ben, just let me live."

Audra tilted her head back and laughed. "Do you really think I want to be saddled with him? No dear. Once you are out of the way, I won't need him any more."

"Then, why?" Nothing made sense to her.

"You've read the journals. Your father was Cal Reeder." Audra shot her a furious glare. "Maybe I should introduce myself. My real name is Audra Reeder. Cal Reeder was my father, too."

January shook her head in disbelief. "We're sisters? Audra, this is crazy! That doesn't explain why you want to kill me."

"I can't take the chance of anyone finding you. Dad invested all the money he made off of Miranda's movies. It's quite a little nest egg. He died last year and

I inherited it all." She seemed to be lost in her story and didn't notice as January eased her way the short distance to a heavy lamp on the table by the letter.

"In the hospital, he told me the whole story about his relationship with the stunning Miranda Call, movie actress extraordinaire," she said disgustedly. "It was all her fault. First, she got pregnant, then she tried to shoot my father." Audra's face paled.

"How ironic that she missed, and killed her beloved Alexander. Dad told me how he struggled to get the gun from Miranda but the gun went off. It wasn't his fault they died."

January shook her head in disbelief. "I don't want anything from you, Audra. Just leave. No one has to know about this."

"It's too late for you. I hate you."

"I don't understand how you can think this will work."

"Ah, that's the best part. My dad kept the news articles about the incident. The Fords' had two children, a boy and a girl. Isn't that funny? Everyone will think you and Ben are brother and sister. Once I destroy the journals, there isn't any possibility of getting caught. "

"No, Audra, you're mistaken. I spoke to Mr. Danvers this evening and told him that I found the journals. I also told him about you father's affair with Miranda. He knows Ben and I are not siblings."

"But...but..."

Suddenly, Calico changed from a lingering breeze to a firm-bodied persona standing at Audra's side. Audra gasped and turned toward January. A question tore at her face. "No! The ghost is just a figment, not real."

While Calico kept Audra's attention, January snatched the large lamp from a trunk near her and hefted it over her head. Suddenly, Ben stood swaying in the doorway as January brought the lamp down on Audra's head.

"I came to save you," Ben said. He had no more then uttered the words when he dropped to the floor, asleep again from the effects of the sleeping pills he had ingested.

January smiled, a look of disbelief crossed her face when she saw that Audra's gun had become dislodged from her grasp and was lying beside Ben. Tears rolled across her cheeks. She wasn't going to die after all. And she was free to love Ben.

CHAPTER 12

Ben struggled awake. The clearer his mind became, the more he felt someone was watching him. He turned his head and a wave of nausea hit him. He swallowed hard and opened his eyes. Slowly the fuzzy blob started taking shape.

Ben's heart fluttered with fear. Disjointed memories from last night floated to the surface of his consciousness. January sat in the window seat, her knees pulled to her chest, the sunlight streaming around her. She looked ethereal. Had she died and become a ghost like Calico?

"Are...are you a ghost now?"

Her eyes rounded. "There's something wrong with us, Ben. I thought you were a vampire and now you think I'm a ghost."

"Whew, I take it you're alive, then."

"Wake-up sleepy head. Those pills Audra gave you have scrambled your mind."

Ben struggled to sit up, but the floral comforter wrapped around his body and made sitting awkward. "How the devil did I get here? The last thing I remember was Audra with a gun pointed at you...you with a lamp in your hands...what happened!"

"I helped you up and you walked here with my help." She smiled, adjusting the bed covers. He must have thrashed around with horrible dreams, nightmarish dreams of her demise.

Ben tried to move, but the twisted covers held him captive. As she watched him struggle for a second she pulled the covers out from under his legs. Free at last, he settled himself in a sitting position against the headboard.

"It was better her than me. Ben, I think she's nuts!"

"Tell me about it. I couldn't believe that she drugged me. But something is missing. What happened?"

January sat beside him and laid her cheek against the top of his head. "After you passed-out on the floor, Sheriff Kinkaid and his deputy burst into the attic with their guns drawn. I thought they were going to shoot me!

Ben swore. "Where's Audra? She's not running around free, is she?"

"Oh no, that nutcase is in jail. I told them what had taken place and when she came around, they handcuffed her and took her off to the Wyland County jail. Actually, it was a letdown. Everything was so intense, then suddenly it was just...over." She rubbed her cheek against his. "I know who our parents are, Ben."

He paled at her words and his dark lashes closed over his eyes. "Our parents? The last thing I remember from last night as I fell into that drugged sleep was Audra telling me that we're siblings. Was she right? You're really my sister?"

January shook her head. "No, I'm not, but it's really complicated, Ben." She told him everything about the journals and Audra's involvement in the situation as she lay beside him stroking his head.

Later, Ben whistled softly under his breath. "This is unbelievable. Audra was using me all the time?"

"I'm afraid so." January took a relaxed breath. "I think we have enough information to do a search of the court house and the newspaper office in Wyland to get verification about our biological parents. Sheriff Kinkaid called earlier. He said Audra confessed to everything. Also, he told me something else. Audra had been coming in the house for nearly a year looking for the journals. She was your vandal."

"Oh my gosh, I feel so stupid. I was playing right into her hands."

"I almost caught her at it, too. Remember that body I found in the attic? That must have been Audra!"

"I'm glad all of this is over because I love you." He pulled his mouth down to hers. His tongue slipped out and feathered softly over her lips. Breaking the kiss, he said, "I want to spend my life with you. Will you marry me?"

January pressed her lips together to keep them from quavering. Tears filled her eyes.

"Hey, Jan. Is that yes or no? I can't tell."

She blinked back the tears. "Yes!"

Ben pulled her close and nuzzled her neck. "Come here you vampire slayer. We're going to spend the morning right here."

The doorbell rang, and January and Ben burst with laughter.

They walked down the stairs hand in hand and met Bennett Sr. pacing across the foyer.

"What in the world has been going on around here? I had coffee at the Grill and everyone was abuzz about the arrest at Pine Gables."

Ben groaned. His father's anger was the last thing he needed today. "I think you'd better follow us to the kitchen, dad. This is going to take a while."

Two pots of coffee later, Bennett, chewing on his bottom lip, looked up at January. "Young lady, you are very, very lucky. Lucky you weren't killed and lucky to be in love with my son."

Ben blinked with surprise. "Thanks, dad. I-I've asked Jan to marry me."

"That's wonderful, son." Bennett said, fiddling with the coffee cup. "I'm glad you were smart enough not to get tangled up with that Audra. She was strange."

January looked at both men. This was a time of change and revelation. She hoped it held true with their relationship. "I hate to change the subject, but I have a problem."

"What?" The men asked in unison.

"Wow! It's not life threatening," she said smiling. "I just need to hire some people to help me around here. Cathy, Jim and I can't do it alone. We need at least three more people. A cook, someone to do the laundry and a host or hostess."

Bennett rubbed his index finger over his chin as he thoughtfully considered her question. "Put and ad in the newspaper for the laundry and cooking positions. I have someone special in mind for the other job."

"Who, dad?" Ben asked.

"Me."

"You?" Ben and January asked in unison.

Ben shook his head with dismay. "Dad, you can't be seri..."

"That's perfect," January interrupted. She leaned forward on her elbows and looked intently at Bennett. "You're exactly the person needed around here. I hope you don't take this the wrong way, but you have a lot of culture and class for this area. I need you to make these executives comfortable here."

January watched how uneasy the men were with each other. Hopefully, this would be the beginning, a way to get father and son working together as equals instead of the father asserting his dominance over his son.

"I think our guests will love your father, Ben. And Ben...with Bennett keeping our guests satisfied, you won't go crazy trying to do the job.

"You think I can't do this, son?" The older man's mouth pulled into a stubborn line.

Ben shook his head. "No, not at all. I don't think that. I'm just surprised, that's all. At least you'll be busy and have another interest besides the agency."

Bennett raised his eyebrows. "That's what you think!"

JANUARY STEPPED OUT the French doors and onto the patio. The rose garden was so fragrant at six in the morning when the sun was beginning to peek over the horizon.

She sat down on the lounge chair and relaxed. This estate had changed so much since her arrival in Garrison in the early spring. She didn't miss the weeds and overgrown bushes that hid the beautiful house, but she did miss Calico.

Ever since that terrible afternoon in the attic, Calico had disappeared. Maybe she'd only been there to guide January to solve the mystery of Alexander and Miranda Ford.

It was time to quit calling the ghost Calico she supposed. She and Ben had spent many hours in the basement of the Wyland courthouse looking through records. But the final piece of information was found in the attic. When January knocked Audra down that night during the struggle in the attic, Audra bumped a photograph keeper. The antique box was lined with a special material to protect photographs from fading.

When January looked through the old photographs, she was shocked to come face-to-face with Calico. The woman, Gabrielle Call, dressed in an old style dress was the exact image of her Calico.

In another area of the attic were old letters, cards and special trinkets given to Miranda from her grandmother, Gabrielle. The orphaned young girl had lived in Wyoming at the mansion and she loved her grandmother dearly and in the end, she had inherited the house after Gabrielle's death.

Apparently, Gabrielle loved Miranda enough to help tell the world about her death.

January's eyes grew heavy. The nightmares where Audra held her captive at gunpoint had subsided since Audra's trial. The charges against her would keep her in prison for a long time. Maybe she would get some mental help while there. Lord knows she could use it.

THE SUN SHONE HOT ON her skin and she arose, and took her cold coffee to the kitchen. "Good morning, Jan," Cathy called to her. "Are you getting excited? Only three hours and you will have a new name."

"New name?" Her eyebrows knitted into a solid line.

Cathy's eyes grew wide. "Well yeah, Cottier."

January shook her head and smiled. "I hadn't thought of it that way. I plan to hyphenate our names. I will be January Mohr-Cottier."

"Hmmm...these new things seem to be a lot more work than the old-fashioned method."

Laughing, January walked toward the foyer at the front of the house. Her mother had decorated the staircase with solid blue ribbons and quaint calico bows. Skipping up the stairs, January turned and looked down into the drawing room to see rows of chairs ready for the guests.

The day flew past in a flurry of activity. January was happy, but a corner of her heart yearned for her great-grandmother to be here for this day.

As the first strains of the Wedding March echoed through the mansion, January gripped her father's hand and tearfully smiled up into his eyes. When they had walked down the steps and reached the foyer, January experienced a tingling sensation that filled her body and announced the presence of Cali...no, Gabrielle. January turned and looked to the top of the stairs. Gabrielle stood there and seemed to be smiling.

January had gone to the other side of reality and back again to find her true love, the love of her life. She took a deep breath and stepped into the drawing room ready to start the rest of her life.

The End
The Author, Bev Haynes

Bev Haynes has created stories for as long as she can remember. She writes about things she really loves such as ghosts, old houses, and romance. The more chilling of her hobbies is ghost hunting with an array of gear found on paranormal television programs. Yes, she has captured orbs, black shadows, and disembodied voices. It's a frightening hobby, but enjoyable as well.

An Aquarius baby-boomer, Bev runs to her writing as a means to escape the realities and stresses of everyday life.

A Wyomingite, she enjoys the great outdoors in an untraditional manner, from the large window in her office. She enjoys spending time with her family and helping others find their way through the publishing jungle.

You can find Bev at:
Facebook: https://www.facebook.com/bev.haynes.73
Twitter: @BevHaynes[1]
Blog: http://authorbevhaynes.blogspot.com/

---

1. https://twitter.com/BevHaynes

The Yellow Bordello will be available soon at your favorite retailer.

The Yellow Bordello

By

Bev Haynes

August 1948

The wind blew something fierce and the air, heavy with moisture, pressed a foreboding awareness into his back and shoulders as he pushed open the curtain and gazed down the street. It was just past sun-up. No one would be hanging around the dilapidated whorehouse this early in the morning. Besides, this old place was on its way out of favor in the community. As far as he knew, only Maggie and Jewel still took in customers. As he dropped the tattered floral curtain, he watched his hand tremble. Damn. He needed to think.

If he took the ladies' clothes and all the woman garbage from the tops of the dressers, everyone would think they all had packed up during the night and left town. That was it, the answer he needed. Excitement surged through his body.

He ambled across the room to the closet and pushed aside the plastic curtain Maggie had strung up over a weighty cord to hide her two dresses hanging in there. At the back, he found a battered suitcase hugging the shadows.

Thirty minutes later, he had one trunk, three suitcases and a pillowcase filled with Maggie's, Jewel's and Fire's personal belongings. He didn't take everything, only enough to make the sheriff think the women had moved to a more welcoming place. However, he had to figure out what to do with all of that junk. He guessed it meant a trip back into the tunnel.

He hadn't meant for any of this to happen. He'd left Maggie's room in the middle of the night, hoping she'd think he was gone. But he had waited...waited until everyone left the building except the women.

He'd wanted to convince Maggie to go away with him. He loved her so much. Observing from the end of the hallway, he'd watched her make her way to the ballroom and then he'd followed her to the balcony where the orchestra had set up back in the heydays of the house. Maggie knelt on the floor, and he watched her take her nightly earnings from a pocket in her robe. Effortlessly, she raised a floorboard, but she shocked him. Withdrawing a Derringer, she turned and pointed it at his heart.

"Magnolia, darlin' what the hell are you doing with that?" he had cried, using her full name instead of his endearing nickname, terrified that she'd really use the gun on him.

She stared at him with eyes round as saucers. "What are *you* doin' here? I thought you were a robber."

"I came to take you away with me." His heart pounded out a staccato of fear when he realized she knew who it was, and she still had the gun pointed at him.

She shook her head slowly back and forth, her curls bouncing against her neck. "Forget it. I wouldn't go with you now if my life depended upon it." She continued to point the gun at him. "I'm not goin'. Now leave me alone."

He lunged toward her and she fell against the railing. At the last instant, before she fell over the edge, their gazes met. Hers were filled with hate.

If only sweet Maggie had left with him...

It took two trips to the basement to lug all that junk down there. He would be the last to see the prostitutes alive. No one knew that a spur off the main tunnel still existed. He had found it accidentally while waiting, night after night. Waiting for the men to leave Maggie's room. He and Maggie had talked for weeks about the life they would have when she left ...until a week ago. That's when she found out he wasn't a wealthy rancher, only a hired hand.

Damn.

It had taken a lot of work to pile the large rocks in front of the plank door. Now he had to move them again. The women's clothing and notions must disappear to have his plan work. He started moving the rocks.

"Help! We're in here! Let us out!"

He could barely make out the muffled sound of female voices screaming in terror. They pounded on the door and the rocks began to move from their attempts to break free. He propped the flashlight in the stones he'd already moved and then swung open the door with one hand while keeping the gun pointed toward the captives.

Three sets of eyes rounded with terror. Swallowing past the greasy lump in his throat, he fired three times and watched with dismay as two bodies dropped. He couldn't believe he was actually doing this.

The older woman, Madam Madeline Brown, Miss Fire they called her, glared at him. "Why are you doing this?" she asked bitterly, her voice steady and demanding. She didn't look down to see if her daughter Jewel was dead or alive.

"I don't have a choice! Maggie is dead because of me."

"You shot Jewel and Lolly! They didn't deserve this." Her voice was a whisper.

He aimed the gun at her chest. "I'm doing you a favor. It's better to go like this than if I left you in here to starve to death."

He pulled the trigger.

Don't miss out!

Visit the website below and you can sign up to receive emails whenever Bev Haynes publishes a new book. There's no charge and no obligation.

https://books2read.com/r/B-A-XCGB-XGXT

BOOKS 2 READ

Connecting independent readers to independent writers.

Also by Bev Haynes

Quilted Hills
In Plain Sight
Amish Heritage
One Amish Autumn
My Amish Rose
Amish At Heart

Standalone
Everlasting Love

About the Author

A Journey Through Words

Bev Haynes has been weaving tales since she could first scrawl words on a small, green-topped desk. Her earliest stories, written in childhood, were the seeds of a lifelong passion for storytelling. In high school, she delighted her friends by crafting narratives starring their favorite musicians and actors as the heroes and heroines, showcasing her knack for creating engaging and personalized tales.

Her career took a pioneering turn at the dawn of the ebook revolution in the year 2000. As a frontrunner in the online publishing industry, Bev quickly established herself as a versatile and innovative author. She has since worn many hats, including that of an editor and, cover artist.

Bev's literary repertoire is as diverse as it is expansive, featuring genres that range from Amish romance and contemporary romance to paranormal romance. Currently, she is channeling her creative energies into a compelling Paranormal Women's Fiction novel, populated by witches, shape-shifters, and vampires.

Living on the sweeping plains of Wyoming near Cheyenne, Bev lives with her supportive husband and their delightful Yorkie. With her children grown and pursuing their own paths, she now enjoys ample time to delve into her writing pursuits and explore new creative horizons.

Bev Haynes continues to enchant readers with her vivid imagination and heartfelt stories, leaving an indelible mark on the literary world.